PAWN

Revenge is just the beginning

Barry Katz

PAWN

Revenge is just the beginning

Copyright 2018 – Barry Katz

PROLOGUE

The brunette stirred.

Her breath was wheezy and her vision blurry as she came to. She just might slip into another comatose state. She whimpered, sucking in her surroundings. She lay on a bed in an unfamiliar room she didn't remember stepping into. Her legs dangled off the side of the bed. A shaky breath slipped out of her mouth and she caught a whiff of alcohol. Had she been drinking? She tried hard to think but there were no recollections of the events leading up to this moment.

She pushed herself off the bed.

That was when she found two men standing a distance away, watching her. They'd apparently been waiting for her to wake up. But who were they? She'd never seen them before and had no memory of how she'd ended up in a room with two strange men, one of which was old enough to be her father.

"Who are you guys?" she asked, her eyes round with suspicion. She swiveled her head in all directions, looking for a clue—anything to give out their location. "Where am I?"

Something didn't seem right.

She rose up from her sitting position.

"Somebody, please help me!" she screamed. She retreated from the men, her eyes fixed on the exit door as she calculated how quickly she could get to it if she made the run for it.

"Easy there, sweetheart," the older man said. "There's nothing to be afraid of. I'm your husband. You fell down and hurt yourself real bad."

He pointed to the other man. "This nice man is a doctor, and he is here to examine you to make sure you're okay."

The supposed doctor smiled at her.

"Go ahead and take off all your clothes, honey," her acclaimed husband urged. "Everything will be okay."

He sauntered to the door and stood in front of it, smashing her dreams of an escape. It was apparent these men weren't who they claimed to be. They could be abductors, or worse, murderers. Either way, her life was at stake. She had to do something—anything.

Barely thinking, she let out a blood-curdling scream.

"Shut that bitch up!" the older man ordered his second. "Now! Hold her still and put your hand over her fucking mouth."

The younger man stood still.

"Do it!" the older man growled. "Goddamn it!"

The brunette stepped backward as the younger man stepped in toward her, his steps tentative. Her eyes were wide with fear. She whimpered as her back met the cold wall.

"Don't hurt me," she pleaded.

The man secured her in his arms, and a scream tore through her mouth. He turned her around so she had her back to him. His hands pressed down on her mouth, muffling her screams. She thrashed around, kicking and wiggling.

The older man approached, his eyes darkened with rage. He wrapped his right hand into a fist and drove it into her stomach. She grunted, collapsing to her knees. The man behind her was apparently shaken. He stepped out of the way and she raised her eyes to see the older man grabbing a lamp. He ripped the

• • •

cord from the wall and smashed it over her head. Blood trickled from her lacerated skull, and another wave of dizziness overwhelmed her, shoving her off the edge of consciousness once again.

But she didn't stay unconscious for long.

When she came to, she found herself laying prone on the floor, with the weight of a man crushing her naked body. It was the same man who'd lied about being her husband. Her legs were spread, opening her to him against her will. He took her from behind, every thrust making her jerk and shudder. He pinned her wrists to the floor on either side of her. His thrusts were hard and unforgiving, rough and brutal, slamming her into the tiles. He filled her to the core, stretching her to his satisfaction. He grunted and moaned, rotating his hips and grinding against her with an intensity that brought an ache to her abdomen. A similar ache found her breasts, and a scream lodged in her throat.

She opened her mouth to let out the scream as he kept pumping her, and a realization that she'd been gagged made her shudder with helplessness. Losing count of time, she lay still underneath him like a log of wood, unable to protest as he alternated between perverted positions, violating her repeatedly.

Not caring about her languidness, he heaved her off the floor and flung her to the bed so she lay supine. He aligned his body with her, nudging her legs open as he lowered himself to her. She tried to clamp her legs shut, but a series of spanks forced them apart. He settled into place, taking her from the front with a raw inhumane passion. Being taken by a wild beast would have been no different. He yanked up her legs and wrapped them around his waist, aiding himself to go deeper. Her sore breasts jiggled with his every thrust. Her stinging nipples led her to a conclusion that he'd bitten them hard while she lay unconscious.

* * *

She flung her head back, crying into the gagging device around her mouth. She was out of breath, losing the will to keep living. Slowly and slyly, she slipped back toward unconsciousness, but each thrust yanked her back to life as he seeded her womb in a relentless display of dominance.

She thought she'd had it all, seen it all.

And when he shoved the barrel of a gun into the raw opening between her legs and squeezed the trigger, she knew this was it.

CHAPTER ONE

It was unlike her to leave her desk messy, but loads of work pressing down on her didn't give her a moment to tidy up the paperwork strewn across her desk. The clicking of keyboard keys and the fluttering of paperwork could be heard as everyone sat in their cubicles, engrossed in their individual work duties. An indistinct conversation filtered through Melissa O'Connell's ears as two co-workers gossiped down the hall. An air conditioner stood just behind her cubicle, and she could hear its tireless buzzing, almost like a white noise. She sighed, hating that she had to be the one nearest to it. The annoying sound would be out of earshot for those on the far end of the office, but she was stuck beside it, with a boss who didn't see a need to fix the faulty fan blades just yet. She couldn't blame him anyway; not when he sat undisturbed in his luxurious office where every installation was fit as a fiddle.

The sound of purposeful footsteps approached as a co-worker walked around her desk to meet a cube-neighbor. Melissa returned her gaze to the words she'd been typing on her desktop. While she typed, her phone lay sandwiched between her head and left shoulder, with half her attention buried into the call she was currently making.

"I know, honey," she said. "We've been through this a thousand times, an' yes!"

She pounded the desk with her fist, and a pin-drop silence followed right after. The chores in the office seemed to have paused. Well, except for the diligent air conditioner behind her.

"Is that what you wanna hear, Chris?" she made an effort to keep her voice down. "Yes, I did! Jesus Christ! I really don't have time for this right now. I'll talk to you later."

Ending the call, she slammed her phone against her desk. Her gaze darted over the top of her cubicle, meeting several pairs of eyes staring in her direction. On cue, they all turned back around so she wouldn't catch them staring. Things had gotten ugly the last time she'd fumed over a meddling colleague sticking his nose where it didn't belong. The office murmured with life as everyone returned to their duties. Everyone but Melissa. She stared at her desktop and the job she'd left undone. And without a will to resume, she propped up her elbows on her desk and clutched her head. Glittery brown hair spilled out on both sides of her face, like a curtain of some sort.

"Everything okay?" a mildly concerned voice asked.

Startled, Melissa lifted her head and found her boss staring at her. He stood some feet away, his arms crossed over his chest. Even in his early fifties, David Liebowitz still had the agility and adroitness of a youth. He was dressed in a smart-fitting ash suit, and underneath it, a white cashmere sweater stood in place of a formal long-sleeved shirt. The round neck of the sweater rode low on his chest, giving some tattoos a chance to peek through.

"Oh!" Melissa said. "Yeah, I'm okay. Just havin' one of those days, ya know?"

David nodded in understanding. "Can I see you in my office?"

"Uhhh...sure." Melissa glanced down at her desktop screen which had faded to black. "Gimme just a sec to finish something up. I'll be right in."

David walked away without another word. Rounding up her typing within the span of five minutes, Melissa thrust into her bag, her hand feeling for her mirror. Finding it, she flipped

* * *

open the plastic lid and held it an arm's length away so she could have a full view of her face. She grimaced at the sight of her rather parched lips and pulled out a pink lipstick from her bag. She applied a thin layer of lipstick, smacking her lips together to spread it evenly. Returning the mirror and lipstick into her bag, she rose to her feet, her gaze finding the rather disheveled state of her blouse. She tugged at the hem of her blouse to put it back in shape. And just before vacating her desk, she undid the top button of her blouse and adjusted her full breasts.

The eyes of her colleagues seemed to follow her as she made her way to the other end of the office where a passageway showed her to David's office. It was natural for them to stare, she knew. She wore a high waist corporate trouser, which clung to her body like a tattoo, closely following every curve and contour of her hourglass figure.

Finding David's door open, she stood in the doorway, watching him as he sat behind his desk, fidgeting with a pen. He looked up at her and waved her over. She stepped into the office, her stride tentative.

David dropped the pen on his desk. "Go ahead and close the door behind you."

Melissa shut the door and took a seat across from him. "If this is about the personal phone calls, I can—"

David raised his hand, cutting her off. "Melissa, this has nothing to do with personal phone calls, performance, nothing like that." A momentary silence trailed his words like a damned punctuation. "You always end up getting the work done and your work is good."

He took a deep breath, and if Melissa didn't know any better, she'd say he was mustering up the courage to deliver his next line. He looked down at the pen on his desk as though conflicted about picking it up again to fidget with it. Melissa sprang back in her chair, brows furrowed as to why he had summoned her. And his awkward pause was not making things easier.

"So what's this all about, then?" she asked.

When he looked up at her again, the sullenness spreading across his face could not be mistaken. "There's no easy way for me to say this. Unfortunately, your position here at J.P.S. is no longer required. Trust me, this was not my—"

A look of disdain washed over Melissa's face. "So, you're laying me off? With all due respect, David, I'd love to know how you determined that *my* position is no longer required. I'm freakin' buried in work every day. This is bullshit, and you know it! Your little pet, Shelly, over there struts in late every day, surfs the net, checks personal email and she's still here? What the fuck?"

Melissa had walked past Shelly on her way to David's office. The frumpy younger woman had been sitting at her desk just outside David's office. Half-asleep and half-reading a copy of *People* magazine, she'd been casually sipping her coffee, completely oblivious to her ringing phone.

"Do you really think this was an easy decision for me?" David leaned in close to Melissa, his voice dropping to a whisper. "Those three weeks were the most incredible three weeks of my life! What happened happened and we promised each other that it wouldn't interfere with our professional lives."

With a huff, he continued, "Look, I have no choice here. With the recent acquisition, we needed to right size. Consider this a favor, sweetheart. You can do better."

Melissa gritted her teeth and shook her head in defiance. She rose to her feet, her palms flat against the desk. "Don't you 'sweetheart' me! You know damn well I have twin boys at home, a mortgage, a car payment, and a worthless husband who thinks selling a bunch of crap on eBay is making a living.

Unemployment pays shit, David! A little notice would have been nice. Go to hell, asshole!"

She stormed out of the office and slammed the glass door behind her, causing the hanging blinds to sway from side-to-side.

***

Melissa bolted out of the building where she'd been working for the past few years. She headed for the parking structure, awkwardly balancing a box of personal belongings with one hand while digging through her purse with the other. Her fingers clasped around a thin slice of cold metal she knew was her car key, and she yanked out the bunch of keys.

She strutted past two day workers sitting at a table in the courtyard, having lunch. She could feel their eyes piercing through her, but she made no attempt to look in their direction.

"Damn, girl!" one of the men called out. "Lookin' good! You need some help with that box?"

"And he don't mean the one you're carrying!" the second man cracked.

Melissa turned to look at the men and they burst into laughter, high-fiving each other. Her stomach twisted into a furious knot as their pathetic images defiled her eyes.

"Hey, amigos!" Her voice stayed calm despite her flaring temper. "I would like nothing more right now than to pull out a gun and blow your fucking brains out! However, I have better things to do with my time, so I'll leave you with a little warning. If I ever see your grimy, filthy, disgusting faces again, I will kill you both! And no, I'm not kidding."

Without waiting for a reaction, she resumed her fast pace toward the parking structure. She noticed though, that she'd left them shaken and short of words.

"Holy shit!" she heard the second man say. "That girl *es loca*! You know what they say, crazy bitches fuck the best!"

"We better get back," the first said.

Rolling her eyes at them, Melissa reached her silver Range Rover and placed the box in the trunk. She ducked behind the steering wheel and started the engine, pulling out of the parking structure and into the streets of Los Angeles. She inched her way through the bumper-to-bumper traffic on the 405 Freeway South. Shoving a cordless bluetooth earbud into her right ear, she dialed a number on her cellphone. While the phone rang on the receiving end, she tapped the wheel, forming a beat.

"Tots 'n' Toddlers, this is Amy," a bubbly feminine voice said into the headset.

"Hey Amy," Melissa said, "it's me, Melissa."

"Oh, hey Melissa! The boys are fine. They're just playing a game in the media room." She paused in thought. "You okay? You don't usually call this early."

Melissa glanced at the time on her car's dashboard. 2:45 p.m. Her eyes were starting to burn with tears, and her throat tightened as she fought against breaking into tears in the middle of a conversation.

"Not really," she said, blinking back her tears. "I'm on my way to pick up the boys. I have the worst headache and my boss just let me go."

"Aw, honey!" Amy's voice dripped with concern. "I'm so sorry to hear that. If there's anything I can do..."

"I'll be okay. Been through a lot worse in my day. Just bad timing, that's all."

"I'll start gettin' the boys ready." Amy's voice rose in pitch as she spoke to her colleague, "Hey, Kim. Can you please round up the twins when you're done with that? Melissa's on her way to pick them up."

"Sure!" Kim's voice was just loud enough for Melissa to hear.

"Thanks, Amy," Melissa said. "I should be there in about fifteen minutes."

"No prob," Amy said. "Drive safe."

Hanging up, Melissa yanked off the headset. The tears she'd been holding back marched out of her eyes. They flooded her cheeks, and her hushed gasps and hiccups filled the air. She sobbed on, oblivious to the loosening traffic. It wasn't until the cars lined up behind her, honked at her, that she realized the cars in front of her had steered forward.

CHAPTER TWO

The smirk on Chris O'Connell's face reeked of deception. He sat at the desk in his home office, his face only inches away from the monitor as he typed on the keyboard. Under the alias of 'Roaming_Cobra,' he exchanged instant messages with 'Satin_Damsel95', a girl whom he only just started messaging. He glanced over his shoulder every now and then as he typed a response to her last message.

His words appeared on the screen. *So, Satin_Damsel95, you ever gonna tell me your real name?*

He leaned back in his seat, gently rocking it back and forth. He glanced at his watch as he awaited her response. His toned biceps and broad chest were in a bid to burst out of his tight-fitting sweatshirt. He never missed a session in his home gym. His daily workout routine was just as important as his breakfast. It was, in fact, the first meal of his day.

The ringing telephone beside him stole his attention. He answered the call.

"Hello." He listened to the person on the other end of the phone, and his eyes stayed fixed on the monitor. "Ummm, she's still at work. Wanna try back in a couple of hours?"

He slapped his forehead in frustration. "Okay. I'll tell her you called."

He hung up the phone just in time to see a new message from Satin_Damsel95 popping up on the monitor. *I don't give my name out to just anyone I meet online, Rob. You could be a psycho for all I know! Is that even your real name?*

* * *

Chris messaged back. *Yeah, it's my real name...*

Satin_Damsel95 responded right away. *Send me your picture. If you're cute, I'll consider.*

Chris messaged back. *I'll send you mine if you send me yours?*

Satin_Damsel95 responded right away. *You first.*

Chris scrambled to find a picture. He grabbed a family portrait from the desk, removed the picture from the frame, and scanned it into the computer.

Another response from Satin_Damsel95 appeared on the monitor. *I'm waiting...?*

Chris typed. *It's coming.*

He watched with glee as the scanned image appeared on the monitor. His wife and four-year-old identical twin boys smiled at him from the picture, oblivious to the fact that he was cropping them out. With his family now out of the picture, Chris was left with a photo of him that was a lot like a passport photograph. But that would do. He sent the picture to Satin_Damsel95, a boyish smile crossing his face as he waited for her response.

Almost immediately, Satin_Damsel95's words appeared on the monitor. *You didn't tell me you were such a hottie! :) How old are you?*

Chris' response appeared. *38. You?*

A new response popped up on the monitor. *You mean to tell me my screen name doesn't give it away?*

Chris' brows twitched as he pondered briefly. And then his eyes twinkled with a realization. He did a quick calculation with her screen name. *23! I'm old enough to be your father.*

Then maybe you should spank me, daddy. I've been a very naughty girl! I'm removing my panties for you right now.

Satin_Damsel95's words caused Chris to shudder with excitement and he groped his hardening dick.

Gulping as he typed his response, he glanced over his shoulders at intervals. Even though he knew Melissa wouldn't be home until evening, he couldn't help his tenseness. She would kill him if she ever discovered his dirty little secret.

Done typing, he hit the enter button. He reread his message as he waited for her to reply. *Shouldn't you be at work or school or something? How do I know you're really who you say you are?*

Satin_Damsel95's response appeared. *It's called P.T.O. and I'm the onefuck-fantasy that married men like you dream about.*

Her second response followed right away. *I know you photoshopped that picture, Rob. It's okay. Married men are safe.*

Chris smiled, then sent his response. *Paid time off, huh? Must be nice. Where's your picture?*

He bristled at the sound of the front door creaking open. His gaze dropped to the time on the monitor. It was barely even 3:00 p.m.

"Chris?" Melissa shouted from the main entrance. "You here? Need some help with the groceries."

Chris scrambled to remove the picture from the scanner and promptly returned it to the frame. He switched off the monitor to conceal his sins.

"Uhhh," he shouted back, his voice somewhat quivering, "hey, honey! I'm in the office finishing up some work. Be right down!"

Collecting himself, he trudged out of the room. He peered at Melissa over the staircase banister as she struggled in the entryway with the twins and some groceries. A thick air of

* * *

guilt camped around him, holding him back from approaching his family.

"You coming down to help or you just gonna stand there and stare at me?" Melissa asked, in a huff.

Chris trotted down the stairs, making his way toward the doorway. Pulling away from Melissa, Alex and Joshua sprinted toward Chris, their booted feet thumping on the floor, and their eyes gleaming with excitement. They'd taken after their mother's sleek brown hair and pointed nose. The only thing they'd taken after their father was his oval face—if that counted at all, considering that Melissa had the same feature.

"Daddy!" Alex and Joshua huffed. "Daddy!"

Chris picked them both up and kissed their cheeks. "How are daddy's lil munchkins doin' today, huh? Daddy missed you both so much!"

Alex and Joshua wrapped their diminutive arms around Chris' neck, squeezing him with affection. Chris watched Melissa's back view as she headed for the kitchen with bags of groceries.

"Daddy, can we stay home with you instead of going to daycare?" Alex asked.

"Yeah!" Joshua said.

"I don't know, slugger," Chris said. "Daddy's gotta work to make sure you guys have everything you need to grow up big and strong! I can't pay the bills if I'm watching cartoons all day, can I?"

"How come?" Joshua asked.

Alex furrowed his brows. "Yeah, daddy. How come?"

Chris chuckled as the boys interrogated him. "You're way too young to understand, fellas. Way too young!" His gaze settled on Melissa as she strutted back into the living room. "You're home early today?"

● ● ●

"Hon', can you please grab the rest of the groceries from the car?" Melissa asked. "I'll explain later when we put the boys down."

"Ummm," Chris said, "yeah, sure."

Melissa smiled at the kids. "Who's up for a snack?"

"Me!" they squealed in unison, darting into the kitchen.

Melissa ruffled Alex's hair as he ran past her. She placed her hand on the small of Joshua's back, ushering him into the kitchen. Chris started toward the car in the driveway, then he looked back at her. Something seemed wrong; she'd never returned from work this early. She'd had her current job for five years, and not once had this happened.

"Everything okay?" he asked.

"Chris!" Melissa said with a raised voice. "I said I'll explain later. Jesus Christ!"

She disappeared into the kitchen, and Chris shrugged one shoulder as he pondered briefly. Exiting the house, he headed for the Range Rover and grabbed the remaining grocery bags from the open trunk. His gaze settled on Mr. Hollingsworth as he hobbled by. The man's wrinkled fingers were wrapped around a cane, and he leaned forward, taking labored steps as though he were weighed down by an invisible burden. An ashen hat sat atop his head, completely covering up an anemic field of white where coarse black hair had once been.

"Hey, Mr. Hollingsworth!" Chris greeted. "How are ya?"

"Hey there, son!" Mr. Hollingsworth said in a feeble voice. A smile squeezed through his age-deformed face. "Would be a lot better if my back didn't hurt like Sam Hill, but at my age, grateful to be alive. How's everything going with your business? You rakin' in the dough?"

"Hardly call it rakin'," Chris said, "but somethin' like that. I'll tell ya something, Mr. Hollingsworth, being self-employed sure ain't all it's cracked up to be."

Mr. Hollingsworth puffed out a laugh. "Yep, I know all about it! Hang in there, kiddo. Don't beat yourself up. You're a sharp guy. Beautiful home, beautiful wife, beautiful kids. What more could you want?"

Chris chuckled. "You're right, Mr. Hollingsworth. When you're right, you're right!"

A momentary silence passed between the two men.

"I better get back inside now," Chris said. "Nice talkin' to ya. Enjoy the rest of your walk."

Mr. Hollingsworth waved him goodbye and resumed his walk. Chris shut the trunk as gently as he could, but with his two hands engaged, it still ended up as a slam. He sighed heavily. The glare of sunlight hit him with its full intensity as he headed back toward his house. He squinted instinctively.

Making his way into the house, he elbowed the entrance door and it clicked shut. An indistinct conversation between his wife and kids sailed into his ears as he advanced toward the kitchen. Joshua and Alex sat at a table, munching on some chips.

Melissa crossed the kitchen to meet Chris. Taking the bags of groceries, she put them away and returned her attention to the food she was warming up in the microwave. Chris stepped in toward her and snaked his arms around her. He turned her around to face him, and she splayed her right palm on his broad chest, tilting her head sideways to escape a kiss as he lowered his lips toward hers. His lips met her neck instead, planting a muffled peck.

A sheepish smile found Melissa's face. "Not in front of the kids, hon."

CHAPTER THREE

Expensive cars rolled down the well-lit streets of Beverly Hills, with restaurants and shops flanking the road. Pedestrians trooped down both sides of the road, the soles of their footwear clapping onto the pavement. The sun shrank back between thick clouds, giving the moon a royal invitation to peek through. Stephanie strolled through town, holding hands with Mitch—a handsome young man whom she'd just starting dating. He was barely an inch taller than her five-foot-eight frame. Stephanie relished the feel of the warm evening breeze rustling her hair, but not so much that it tousled it.

Her ears picked up a rattling sound, and her eyes zeroed in on a ragged man as he blurred into view from the other end, frantically wheeling an empty shopping cart. Hunched over, he steered the cart toward a man walking past him. The screeching of tires on the asphalt and the shuffling of feet against the pavement muted out the man's words. But the sight of him holding up a photograph and his eagerness to hold the other man's attention told Stephanie just what she needed to know— he had lost something dear to him and was in dire need of help.

Stephanie's hand tightened around Mitch's as she watched the other man walk away without slowing his stride to look at the needy man. The needy man held out the photograph, whirling it around and flashing it in people's faces, but no one would spare a glance. Overgrown stubbles framed the man's slim face, making him look a tad older than he really was. But Stephanie could bet on it that he was only old enough to father a child half her age.

* * *

Now within range, Stephanie could hear the man's voice.

"Excuse me," she heard him say. "Excuse me. Have you seen my dog?"

She was close enough to see the picture the man was holding. On it was a regal looking Pit Bull Terrier sitting on a rug and staring up at the camera.

"I don't want any money," the man said to a woman. "Please, I just need to find my dog!"

But the woman ignored him just like everyone else.

Stephanie tugged Mitch's arm. "Aww, sweetie! It's a pittie! I love pitties! We have to help."

Mitch squirmed with unwillingness. "We're late for our dinner reservation, babe. We really need to get going."

The man was in front of them now, gripping the picture with one hand, and his other hand tight around the empty cart. His eyes brimmed with tears. "Please! Nobody else will help me. No one will even talk to me. Rex is my only reason for living. I was robbed last night. They took everything! I don't care about my stuff, I just need my friend back. Please help!"

Staring into the dog's face brought a hushed calmness upon Stephanie. Images of a smaller pit bull terrier darted across her memory. She remembered him jumping into her bed and licking her face whenever she overslept. The pup would always wag his tail at her whenever she returned from work, and she'd ruffle his fur and pet him.

She soothed the man with her soft gaze. "We're gonna help you, okay? Mine passed away during routine surgery a few months ago. I know what you're going through. Everyone in this town hates them. They are always discriminated against, but ya know what? They are God's creatures too, and with love, they love back. We will help you find Rex. I promise."

* * *

Overcome by emotion, the man wept and collapsed to his knees. Stephanie winced at the sound of the man's knees colliding with the hard concrete, but the accompanying pain seemed nonexistent to him.

"I don't know how to thank you enough," he said, his words distorted by overflowing emotions. "I have nothing to offer you, just my appreciation. God bless you both."

"Excuse us for a moment," Mitch said to him and pulled Stephanie aside, giving her shoulder a firm grip. "Steph, I know we just met, but uh...what are you doing? I wanna help him as much as you do, but we can't promise him anything. I mean, how do we even get in touch with the guy if we find the dog? Let's be sensible here."

Stephanie turned to face the man. "Where do you live?"

He looked between Stephanie and Mitch. "Here on the streets."

The look in the man's eyes became more sullen, and then he lowered his head. She gave him the once-over, and it struck her that she could have guessed from the start that he was homeless, but her attention had been fixed on the picture the whole time.

"Sorry," she backpedaled, groping for a more suitable question. "Stupid question. Blonde moment. I mean, where can we find you? If we find your dog, where can we find you?"

She watched him keenly as he rose to his feet.

With a blast of blue and red lights flashing on its rooftop, a police car screeched into view. The homeless man's eyes went round with a shuddering fear and a gasp tore through his lips. Abandoning his shopping cart, he darted off, his long-sleeved shirt billowing in the cool evening breeze. A middle-aged male officer burst out of the police car and bolted after him.

A surge of adrenaline flooded Stephanie's veins at the abruptness of the chase, and her heart pounded hard against her chest as she tried to make sense of the situation. Mitch and several pedestrians stood in awe as well. They watched until the duo was out of sight.

"What the fuck was that all about?" Mitch asked. "We're in Beverly Hills, for Christ sake!"

"Exactly!" Stephanie paused, steadying her pacing heart. "They're not welcome here. Cop is probably just tryin' to scare him away."

Visibly shaken, Mitch shook his head as though to rid himself of the image of what he'd just seen. "I don't know about him but that kind of shit scares *me* away! Let's get out of here. I don't have a good feeling about this."

Stephanie's gaze stayed fixed on the picture which had fallen into the cart as the homeless man sprinted off. She glanced over her shoulder at the cart as Mitch led her in the opposite direction. Their pace was a tad faster than the casual stroll they'd started off with.

"Let's take the alley," she suggested. "It's faster."

They turned left into a dimly lit alley, leaving the squealing and screeching of tires behind them. Trudging forward, their shod feet sloshed on the wet and slick pavement. The alleyway stretched on until forever, with the receding sun emitting its soft glow on the other end, bathing the overreaching granite walls in the last of its beams. Stephanie gripped Mitch's arm, gluing herself to him. It had been ages since she last passed an alleyway at night. There were notorious stories of a showy display of lawlessness between these walls once it was nighttime, and the last thing she wanted was to be on the receiving end.

"I don't really like alleys," Mitch said.

"Me neither," Stephanie said. "But we're running late and a short cut wouldn't hurt."

A pair advancing toward them caught her eye. She lowered her gaze, more interested in the four legged creature than in the man sporting an Adidas baseball cap. With his right hand, he gripped one end of the leash tied around the pit bull's neck. Stephanie locked eyes with the man just as he began to walk past with his dog.

"Is your dog friendly?" she asked.

The man stopped, and his dog mirrored his move. He seemed to be in his forties.

"Oh yeah!" he said.

Hooking a wisp of blonde hair behind her left ear, Stephanie bent over to greet the dog. The non-threatening animal wagged his tail, apparently enjoying the attention.

She patted his head, briefly running her fingers through his fur. "Hey, big guy! What's your name?"

The dog licked her face in response.

Chuckling, she gave his head a final pat and stood upright, her gaze never leaving him. "I had one just like him. Well, not so big, but friendly like him."

"His name is Rex," the man said in a husky voice typical of a heavy drinker. "My best bud in the whole entire world!"

Stephanie's face contorted with confusion. She turned toward Mitch, and his expression was no different.

"This is gonna sound really strange," Mitch said to the man, "but some homeless guy just stopped us and showed us a picture of your dog. He said the dog was stolen from him."

The man grimaced. "That fucker has been pulling this shit for weeks. Gets nice folks like you to hand over their hard earned cash. It's a scam and if I ever catch that son-of-a-bitch—"

Stephanie and Mitch bristled at the sound of an unmistakable click behind them. They knew for a fact that they

* * *

23

had additional company, and the sound they'd heard was a lot like the cocking of a gun. Simultaneously, they turned around to confirm their fear. A startled gasp escaped Stephanie's lips as she stood face-to-face with two stony-faced thugs. The shorter of them had his fingers wrapped around a gun's handle. At first, it seemed like he aimed the gun at them both, but a second look at his aim revealed Mitch's head as the sole target.

"No," Stephanie muttered to herself, disbelief washing through her.

This isn't happening, she thought. *This isn't happening.* Her inner voice morphed into a silent scream.

From her peripheral vision, she could see Mitch raising his hands in surrender. Unarmed and outnumbered almost two-to-one, surrendering was the only reasonable thing they could do.

"Please, don't hurt us," she begged.

Following Mitch's lead, she raised her arms above her head as well. Her entire body had grown rigid with fear and her hands trembled in midair.

The taller thug grabbed Stephanie. Twisting her arms behind her with one hand, he clamped down on her mouth with his other hand. The man with the dog sauntered into eyeshot, a look of approval swirling in his eyes as he regarded the thugs. A wordless conversation seemed to ensue between them. Apparently, he was the ringleader and this was all a setup—one she'd led her date right into. They should never have taken the shortcut, but it was all too late to turn back now.

Calmly surveying the scene, the ringleader lit a cigarette, took a drag and puffed out a ring of smoke. He circled the scene, with Rex closely behind him, the rather short leash forcing him to follow the man's every step. "Well well," the ringleader said. "What do we have here?"

"Please, man," Mitch pleaded through an apparent lump in his throat, "we don't want any trouble. My wallet's in my back pocket. Just take what you want and let us go. We won't go to the cops, I swear."

The ringleader took another drag of his cigarette, his poise composed and unhurried. He walked over to Mitch and blew smoke directly into his face. Mitch winced, narrowing his eyes to keep out the smoke.

"Ya know what the problem is with people like you?" the ringleader asked. "You talk too fucking much! Never know when to keep your goddamn mouth shut."

Stepping out of the way, the ringleader motioned for the shorter thug to pull the trigger.

"No!" Stephanie screamed, but the hand pressing down on her mouth muffled her voice. She fought against him to break free. There had to be something she could do to save Mitch. But the robust man restraining her barely even twitched in response to her feeble attempts.

The shorter thug pulled the trigger, and Mitch's eyes flew open just in time to see a single shot rocketing straight into his forehead. He dropped dead on the pavement. Blood seeped out of the sizzling entry hole in his head and formed a puddle around him.

Still restrained by the thug behind her, Stephanie cried in silence. Unforgiving tears formed a cold trail down her cheeks and dangled along her jawline. The ringleader handed over the leash to the shorter thug in exchange for the firearm. Holding the gun behind him, he approached Stephanie, and she shuddered with his every move.

He halted only inches away from her. "Now that you know we mean business, sweetheart, you will do as I say. First thing you're gonna do is keep your mouth shut. You go to the cops, we come after you. We ain't gonna kill ya, but you'll wish that we did. Understand?"

Stephanie nodded in agreement. Pallid with fear, she could barely look him in the eye.

"Good!" He nodded at the thug restraining her. "You can let her go now."

The thug released her from his death-grip and she massaged her now aching wrists. That thug had gripped her wrists so hard he'd disrupted the flow of blood.

"Don't think I don't know where to find you," the ringleader said, his cold stare burning into her. Allowing a transitory silence to pass between them, he added, "Stephanie."

Stephanie's eyes widened, and a sudden chill flooded her insides, making her go numb. The man before her was way more than just a random stranger. His knowledge of her could only mean one thing—he'd had her under surveillance. But why would he? Why would anyone? And for how long had he been watching her?

She peered into his face to reconcile his image to that of a man she might have seen at some point in her life. She ran her eyes all over his features, but nothing seemed to ring a bell. Stephanie's fright escalated. Who was this man? And most importantly, what did he want?

Deep in thought and still as a concrete wall, she watched him take possession of Rex while the two thugs heaved Mitch's lifeless body off the ground. They carried his body to a black limousine, and the trunk popped open. Shoving the body into the trunk, they shut the door and hopped into the vehicle.

This was the last Stephanie would see of her newfound love interest.

Her bitter reality sliced through her like a double-edged sword, expelling another round of tears from her eyes. Willing the tears to halt, she tried to focus on the license plate, but her blurred vision could barely even make out the first letter on it. The letter looked a lot like an uppercase 'J', or did it?

* * *

"For your sake, let's hope we never meet again." The ringleader threw his cigarette to the ground and held out Rex's leash to Stephanie. "You can have him."

Stephanie gripped the leash with shaky hands. Pulling away from her, the ringleader slid into the limousine and it sped off just after he shut the door.

Feet hammered the ground toward Stephanie. But she stood unmoving. It wasn't until the person blurred into her vision that she saw it was the same police officer who'd chased after the homeless man. Gun drawn, he glanced at her, his gaze momentarily slipping toward Rex. Approaching with caution, he cast his gaze around to take in the surroundings.

The officer returned his focus to Stephanie. "It's okay, I'm not gonna harm you. Have you seen a homeless guy run through here?

He glanced around again. The puddle of blood on the ground caught his eye and he shone his flashlight on it—the sky had darkened dramatically, making it seem like Stephanie had been here for hours.

The officer spun on his soles, panning the alleyway with his flashlight. He found nothing. He turned toward Stephanie, searching her face with the flashlight. She barely blinked. She stared off into space, letting the officer's image fade into a hazy outline.

"Wanna tell me what this is all about?" the officer asked.

Stephanie felt a strain on Rex's leash as he barked at the officer. Still, she refrained from uttering a sound.

CHAPTER FOUR

"I'll be down in a sec," Melissa shouted to Chris who sat alone at the dining room table. She'd gone upstairs with the kids and Chris had spent the past few minutes waiting for her to come serve dinner.

He plucked a knife from his place setting and spun it around in circles. "No worries, take your time!"

Vacating his seat, he headed for the kitchen where he snuck out a bottle of booze from a cabinet. He took a swig, relishing the taste of it as it imprinted a hot trail down his throat. He returned the bottle to its place and proceeded back to his seat at the dining room table. It took a few more moments for Melissa to join him for dinner.

She slid onto the chair across from him. "Sorry about that. They did not want to go to sleep!"

"Have they eaten already?" Chris asked.

"Yeah, I gave them some mac and cheese while you were in the shower." She served herself a plate of food. "If you wanna hand me your plate, I'll dish up for you."

Chris complied, watching her keenly as she served him some food.

"I was let go today," she said in a nonchalant voice.

Chris choked as he took a sip of water. "Are you serious? Holy shit! Business has been slow for me. Not good timing!"

"Is it ever good timing, Chris?" She shook her head without giving him a chance to respond. "Let's say our prayers. I'll start looking for jobs online tonight."

Chris offered a short prayer and they dug into their meals. While Chris ate, his mind darted back to his unfinished conversation with his online heartthrob. He wanted nothing but to log on and check for her response to his last message.

He bet it was a combination of words that would give him a boner. She had probably even sent him a picture. He had an unwavering feeling she was just as hot as her screen name made it seem. Well, he was just a click away from finding out. Or so he thought.

With a smirk, he shoved a spoonful of food inside his mouth.

***

The faint sound of the living room television flipping through football channels filled Melissa's ears as she unloaded the plates from the dishwasher into the cabinet. At least, the sound was barely loud enough to make it up the stairs and disturb the kids' slumber. Chris was a fast learner—although not very fast. It had taken countless nighttime arguments for him to adapt to turning down the television volume at night. The telephone in the kitchen rang, and Melissa wiped her hands with a clean towel.

"I'll get it!" she shouted out to Chris. She could already imagine him scrambling toward the kitchen to get the phone. She answered the call. "Hello."

"Hey it's Barbara," the caller said.

"Hey, Barbara!"

"Did I catch you at a bad time?"

"Nope, just putting away the last of the dishes. What's up?" Melissa caught a glimpse of the clock which read: 8:30 p.m.

"Was thinking you'd drop by after work to pick up the package," Barbara said.

Melissa touched her temple. "Oh, that's right! I'm so sorry, I completely forgot! I'll send Chris over to pick it up."

"He better get his ass over here asap!" Barbara said.

"You got it!" Casting her eyes on the doorway, Melissa pulled the phone away from her ear and shouted out to Chris, "Hey, Chris. Can you come here, please?"

She returned the phone to her ear. "Thanks, Barbara."

"I suppose the kids are asleep," Barbara said.

"Mmmm hmmm," Melissa said.

"Tell them grandma said hi. I'll drop by to see them sometime soon. Have a great night."

"You too, buh-bye." Melissa hung up and placed the last of the dishes in the cabinet.

Chris stood in the threshold. "You need me?"

Melissa whirled around to face him as he stepped into the kitchen. "Yeah, that was your mom. I was supposed to stop off on my way home and pick up a package that arrived there for you. Can you please swing by right now? She's expecting you."

"A package?" he asked, his voice slurry. He stretched his muscles. He must have dozed off at some point.

"Yeah," Melissa said. "A package. You expecting something?"

"Uhhh, no." Chris clicked his tongue, mulling things over. "Why was it sent..."

He relaxed his attention as a realization seemed to dawn on him.

"Oh," he said. "I know what it is!"

"What is it?" Melissa asked.

• • •

"Something for work. I ordered it a while ago." He paused for a breather. "Forgot about it."

"Why did you have it sent to your mom's house?" Melissa asked.

"Ya know..." He scratched his head, trying to come up with a coherent explanation.

Melissa regarded him with narrowed eyes.

"I can't remember now," he said, shrugging one shoulder. "Maybe we were out of town or something. I didn't want to chance it getting lost."

"Chris, we haven't been out of town in forever-and-a-day," Melissa pointed out, casting him a wary gaze. "Get with it."

Chris laughed. But the laugh got nowhere near his eyes, so Melissa knew he'd faked it.

"I'm sure there was a reason," he said. "I must be getting old."

He grabbed a bunch of keys, a cellphone and a wallet from the kitchen counter. He seemed a tad nervous around Melissa, but she dismissed the thought. She concluded she was overanalyzing things. Her job termination had to do with this, she was sure of it.

"I'll be back," Chris said with a peck to her right cheek.

Melissa cracked him a weak smile. Returning her smile, he walked away. The front door clicked shut as he exited the house. Melissa gazed out the window, her eyes brimming with concern. She could hear the car engine roaring to life, and shortly after, the fading noise announced Chris' departure.

Melissa vacated the kitchen and mounted the stairs to the top floor. She walked past her kids' room and thought of checking on them. But no sooner had she made the decision than she decided against it. The opening and closing of the door might interrupt their slumber. It had taken forever to put them to sleep. She couldn't stand tackling it all over again, especially in her current state of mind. No sounds made it through from the other side of the door, so she concluded the twins were sound asleep.

She strode to her room and shut the door behind her. She'd had a hectic day and was looking forward to the comfort sleep had to offer. But that would have to wait. First, she would try to find jobs online. There was no harm trying. Besides, she'd gotten most of her past jobs online, so there was probably another one waiting for her and she only had to reach out to it.

She took off her garment, flung it onto the bed and gawked admiringly at herself in the mirror. She unhooked her bra and piled it on her blouse. Her gaze circled her breasts; they were almost as perky as they'd been before she had Joshua and Alex. She slipped down her panties and, stepping out of them, she topped up the pile of clothes on her bed with the flimsy cotton fabric.

Flashes of windflaw caused the curtains to billow and flap, earning Melissa's attention. She sighed, hating that she'd forgotten to shut the curtains before getting unclad. She'd be damned if a stalker lurked in the shadows feasting on her stark nakedness. She crossed her breasts with her left hand and approached the open window. Strands of hair danced across her face, obscuring her vision. She lifted her non-dominant hand toward her hair, and just as she pushed the hair behind her ear, she sighted something outside—a pair of binoculars was fixed on her, and behind it was an adolescent boy watching her with his mouth agape.

"You little pervert!" Melissa lashed.

The boy scurried off into a dark corner before Melissa could register his face. She drew the curtains and threw on a bathrobe. Cellphone in hand, she headed for the home office. The door creaked open as she let herself in. It'd been forever since she last visited the home office. But it was the exact opposite with Chris. This was his second most frequented room

• • •

besides the gym, so he couldn't be oblivious to the squeaky door hinges. She would have him do something about it in the morning. Hopefully, a little bit of grease would do.

She felt around the wall for the light switch. Finding it, she switched on the light and scanned the room. Her face contorted with disgust at the sight of Chris' computer glasses amidst a clutter of seldom used books on the desk. Her first guess was the books had been there for eons. A teacup sat in a flat plate beside the computer on the desk, and scattered across the plate were crumbs of what might have been pizza.

"What a freakin' mess!" she muttered.

She sat in the desk chair in front of the computer monitor, and reached across the desk to grab the telephone. She dialed a number.

"Hey," she said into the phone, "it's me! What website did you use to find your job at the bank?"

"*Indeed* did it for me," the girl on the phone said. "It's a great site."

"That's right!" Melissa said. She'd actually considered the website her first option. "Okay, thanks!"

"Anytime, Mel."

Melissa hung up. Staring at a blank screen, she moved the mouse around in circles. Nothing happened. She pushed the power button on the monitor, letting out a sigh as a green light flicked on.

She sighed. "Why the hell was the monitor turned off? God, I hate computers!"

The last correspondence between Chris and a certain Satin_Damsel95 faded into the screen. Melissa hadn't intended to read their entire instant message chat even as it lay exposed before her, but when she caught the vibe of licentious behavior between the two, she didn't have much of a choice.

* * *

Melissa glanced through the electronic conversation, and even as she witnessed the birth of an affair between her husband and the online woman, an eerie calmness and lack of emotion draped her like swaddling blankets.

Scrolling down, the cursor arrived at the final entry from Satin_Damsel95 which read: *My picture is on the way! Gotta run now. Someone is at the door. Catch ya later, handsome!*

Melissa's blank stare hovered over an unread email from Satin_Damsel95. She clicked on it and downloaded two attachments. She opened the first attachment; it contained the picture of a beautiful blonde in her late twenties modeling a summer dress. Her face held a seraphic smile capable of melting snow.

A smile of contentment graced Melissa's face as her steady gaze skimmed along the girl's body. She opened the second attachment and a second picture popped up on the monitor. It was a picture of the same girl, only nude this time. She lay on her side on a flowery-sheeted bed, with her right elbow propped up on the bed, while her left hand rested on the side of her curvaceous ass in a seductive pose. Her pussy was clean-shaven, and Melissa knew the sight of it would cause Chris' perverted mind to explode into a million shards of desire.

Melissa leaned in closer, digesting every square inch of the body. A body like hers could seamlessly give her an appearance in Playboy.

"Wow!" Melissa sat paralyzed for a moment.

Her phone rang, jarring her from a mesmerized trance. Chris' name was stamped on the screen. Calm and composed as though she hadn't just caught him cheating, she answered the call.

"Hey, honey," Chris said.

"Hey," Melissa replied. She could hear a fast-paced rap song emanating from the car stereo.

• • •

"I'm gonna stop off at the drug store," Chris said. "My throat's feeling a bit scratchy. Ya need anything?"

Melissa tapped the mouse as the monitor started fading to black. "Actually, I do! Pick me up some Midol. I have really bad cramps and I'm all out."

"Can you emasculate me just a little more?" Chris said, a tiny smile evident in his voice. "Just kidding. You can pick me up some Preparation-H next time you're at the market."

He laughed patronizingly.

"I buy it all the time," Melissa said, still staring at Satin_Damsel95's nudity. "It's good for wrinkles."

"I've heard that," Chris said. "Okay, sweetie, see you in a bit."

The line went dead. Melissa tore the phone away from her ear and glanced sideways at it. "Bye to you too!"

She dropped the phone on the desk and returned her attention to the computer screen. She mounted her ten fingers on the keyboard, ready to send a message to Satin_Damsel95.

Using Chris' alias, Melissa's words appeared on the monitor. *Hey, beautiful! Sorry I left so suddenly... I had an emergency downstairs.*

She clicked 'send', and then she typed again. *The pictures you sent me are breathtaking. I can't stop thinking about you.*

She sent that as a second message. A cynical grin spread across her face as she typed the next message. *You mentioned something about P.T.O. Where do you work? My sister was laid off and really needs a job. If you know of anything, please let me know!*

And then she wrapped it all up. *Sweet dreams, pretty girl.*

Her desperation steadily built up as she watched the screen in expectation of the girl's reply. "Rob, huh?" An eerie grin

• • •

36

washed over her face. "It's amazing how things sometimes work in your favor."

CHAPTER FIVE

A yellow Lamborghini pulled up to the curb at the valet parking lot of a steakhouse, and behind the steering wheel sat a sophisticated sixty-year-old Jim Powers. He was the C.E.O of Jim Powers Securities, a time-tested financial institution facilitating the buying and selling of securities, and so far he'd made a great reputation for himself and his firm. From the rearview mirror, he sighted David Liebowitz's silver Porsche Carrera GT pulling up behind him. Jim stepped out of his Lamborghini and started toward the restaurant. His stride was elegant and unhurried as though he had all night.

He occupied an empty booth by the window, an aura of confidence surrounding him. Some women in their early thirties kept glancing his way, and even though he found them attractive, he paid no attention to them. It didn't take long for a young bartender to walk over to Jim's table.

The bartender placed a cocktail napkin in front of Jim. "Bombay Martini...straight up...two olives?

"Am I really that predictable?" Jim asked.

"Predictable enough to know I'd see you here tonight," the bartender said. "You're like clockwork, Jim."

They exchanged familiar smiles.

"Johnny Walker Blue," Jim said, "...rocks. Make it a double. How's that for predictable?"

The bartender let out a soft, almost musical laugh. Jim watched David as he strode in, his gaze traveling the length and breadth of the restaurant in search of Jim's booth. Their eyes met and David ambled over, taking the seat across from him.

"Steve-O!" David addressed the bartender. "Still slingin' bottles for a living, huh?" He scoped out the beautiful women. "You gay, son? You're surrounded by all of this and I've never once seen you make a move."

The bartender scoffed. "Difference between you and me, I don't need to make any moves. Pour on the heavy side and everything falls into place. Now what's it gonna be, sweet cheeks? A Shirley Temple?"

"First order of business." David pointed to a booth. "That table over there in the corner—send them your finest bottle of Dom."

Jim followed David's gaze, his eyes settling on three beautiful women enjoying drinks and appetizers while flirtatiously peering at men who were apparently well-to-do. One of them—a redhead—seemed particularly sultry. Her off-the-shoulder dress flashed more cleavage than decency allowed, and her crossed legs flashed even more skin. She threw her head back, laughing over a joke said by her friends. She circled her glass of wine around with her hand, and with a casual turn of her neck, her eyes found Jim's table. She waved at them, then turned back to her friends.

But Jim hadn't missed the come-hither look in her eyes, and he knew David had seen it too.

David smirked, looking up at the bartender. "The redhead in the middle, get me her name and number. Second order of business. Surprise me, but don't be a fucking pussy! I've had a rough day."

"Do you really think this is a good night for surprises?" The bartender grinned cynically as he walked away to get their drinks.

David turned toward Jim, his calmness whooshing away. "What the hell is he talking about?"

"Relax!" Jim said. "He's just messing with you. Stop being so fucking paranoid."

The two men glanced at the bartender who'd begun mixing their drinks at the counter.

"I didn't think you'd go through with it today," Jim said.

"I didn't exactly have a choice," David said.

"She knows something, David," Jim said. "We couldn't afford to take a chance."

The bartender strode back to them with a silver tray bearing their drinks. He transferred the drinks to their table.

"The way she's been looking at me lately, familiarity with disdain. Almost like something's coming back to her." Jim sipped his drink. "She used to pass me in the hall with a smile. It's been different lately. Seems like she's starting to remember things. I don't need her to remember things." He took another sip of his drink. "And neither do you.

David pondered for a moment, and then he gazed at the drink in front of him. His head shot up toward the bartender. "Hey, Steve! What is this pink shit?

The bartender flashed Jim a 'do-something-with-him' look.

"David, pick up the fucking shot glass and drink it!" Jim said. "You told him to surprise you and that's what he did."

David reluctantly picked up the glass, his gaze burning into the pink liquid inside of it. He looked up at the bartender gleefully watching him. With a frown, he looked back at the drink. He squeezed his eyes shut as he took a sip.

David coughed, his eyes prying open. "I said surprise me, not kill me!"

The bartender leaned in toward David, his eyes taking a darker hue. His voice was barely a whisper as he spoke, "It's too late." He glanced at his watch. "You've got about two minutes."

David instinctively leaned back into his seat, away from the bartender. He looked across the table at Jim who sat quietly, looking anywhere but in his direction as though he'd suddenly become invisible.

"What the—" David said.

The bartender erupted into laughter, cutting David off. He straightened his spine. "I'm just shittin' ya!"

"Jesus Christ! Fucker!" David wiped off some sweat which had started to gather on his left brow.

"It's on the house, buddy!" the bartender said. "I'll get you your usual."

Jim set down his drink and rose to his feet. "Excuse me. I'll be back."

He headed into the men's room, passing a bathroom attendant—who was also in his sixties—wiping the counter tops and neatly aligning an array of personal hygiene items. Jim proceeded to do his business at the urinal.

"Excuse me, sir," the bathroom attendant earned Jim's attention. "You Jim Powers?"

"Who wants to know?" Jim asked.

"A gentleman who wishes to remain anonymous has a message for you," the bathroom attendant said.

Jim zipped his fly. While he buckled his belt, he made his way toward the sink. Done with his belt, he adjusted his pants and turned on the faucet. The bathroom attendant hovered over him. Jim wet his hand and looked around for a soap.

"Here you go, sir," the bathroom attendant said, "allow me."

● ● ●

Jim turned toward him and found him offering a soap. "That's okay, thank you."

"Can I interest you in a paper towel?" the bathroom attendant asked after Jim had soaped his hands.

Jim rinsed his hands, his eyes fixed on the bathroom attendant. "Have we met before?"

"No, sir," the bathroom attendant said. "This is my first night."

Jim gave him a once-over. "Where's Leroy?"

"I don't know, sir," the bathroom attendant said. "Some folks said he went back to Mississippi, but I ain't never met him before."

"Sometimes people disappear without a trace. One day they're here...next day...poof, they're gone! I don't think you wanna be one of those people." Jim shook his hands dry. "Do ya?"

"Uhhh...no, sir." The bathroom attendant fidgeted.

"The gentleman who asked you to deliver a message to me..." Jim pulled out a wad of cash from his pocket and peeled off a crisp one-hundred-dollar bill. "Did you notice anything..." He paused, groping for the right words. "...unusual about him?"

"Well, sir..." the bathroom attendant mused, "he had a real big scar on his forehead. He had real bad breath too. I offered him a mint, but—"

That was just what Jim needed to know. He placed the one-hundred-dollar bill in the bathroom attendant's pocket.

"Get yourself something nice, huh? You're a good man." Jim patted him on the shoulder and headed for the exit.

"You have a nice evenin' now," the bathroom attendant said in a high-pitched voice, "ya hear?"

"You do the same, Julius," Jim said. "Pleasure doing business with you."

He waltzed out of the men's room with a wry smile, leaving the bathroom attendant utterly confused as to how he knew his name.

• • •

44

CHAPTER SIX

A glossy black limousine hopped down a slopey road leading to a gigantic gate. It halted just in front of the gate. A crooked aluminum sign hung in the distance, and on it was the inscription: *Heavenly Meadows Pet Cemetery.* The sign cast a dark shadow across the unpaved road, momentarily cutting through the moon's glimmer.

Gus McCain, the infamous ringleader from the alley, sat on the plush white seat of the luxurious vehicle, crossing his legs at the knees. He still had his favorite ball cap enclosed around the top of his head. His eyes were fixed on the window, staring out into the thick blackness of the night. His henchmen, Jesse and Rubin, sat quietly across from him as though they were seated for an interview.

Impatience started to peek through as Gus waited for the gate to be opened. He tapped his fingers on his left knee, forming a rhythm. A man stepped out of the shadows from the other side of the gate. Cloaked in black, he kept his identity a mystery as he threw open the two sides of the gate for the limo to pull in. He shut the gate behind them.

Frankie, the middle-aged driver, parked behind a 1977 Chevy Caprice, and Gus approached the Chevy right after departing from the limo. Felipe, a Hispanic man in his thirties, sat behind the wheel. He was dressed in a green uniform. He leaned into the chair with his head tilted to the right, in the direction opposite Gus'. Once there, Gus banged the window. Felipe acknowledged him with a jolt and hopped out of the vehicle.

● ● ●

"*Hola*, Gus!" Felipe said in a jutting Hispanic accent.

Gus clicked his tongue, his disapproval evident. "Pal, you're in America now. English, please!"

"*Si!*," Felipe said. He reconsidered his word, a look of frustration crossing his face. "I mean yes, *señor*! Uhhh...yes, sir. I mean Gus!"

"What the fuck was that?" Gus snickered. "It's alright, Felipe. I don't speak good English either."

He patted Felipe on the shoulder, lit a cigarette, and cast his gaze around the scene in a quick surveillance. There was no one in sight. A short distance away, moldy tombstones protruded from the ground in neat rows, with eerily tall trees shrouding them from the moonlight. Gus sighted a lone shed on the other side.

His scrutinizing gaze flickered back to Felipe. "You got everyone out of here, right? Everyone go home?"

"Yes," Felipe was quick to answer. "I close the gate and tell everyone we have maintenance tonight. I just unlock the gate for you five minutes ago. The man who let you in is our security guard. He's okay."

"Alright," Gus said. "Same thing as last time. You need us to pull up closer to the shed?"

He looked over to the shed again. It was large, blending into the darkness, except for a dim light spilling out of the open window—a window barely large enough to suck in the moonlight. A wooden sign preceded the entrance. The sign read: *Incinerator. Employees only beyond this point.*

Felipe looked over to the shed as well. "I think we're okay if your friends help carry him there."

"What? And get blood everywhere?" Gus shot Felipe a disbelieving look. Cigarette dangling from his mouth, he placed his hand on Felipe's shoulder. "Pal, if you're gonna start walkin' on our side of the fence, you're gonna have to learn how to cover your tracks. You get sloppy, you end up behind bars."

He looked around—in search of what exactly, he had no idea. But when he spotted a wheelbarrow placed against the fence, he knew that would do.

He pointed to the wheelbarrow. "Go grab that wheelbarrow over there."

Felipe complied.

"Jesse!" Gus yelled, facing the limo, "Rubin! Get the fuck out of the limo and help over here! I'm not paying you to sit on your lazy fat asses!"

Jesse and Rubin reluctantly exited the limo. They stood facing Gus, waiting for his next line of orders.

"Hey!" Gus shouted at the driver, "Frankie, pop the trunk, will ya?"

Gus edged closer to the trunk as it popped open. He looked inside of it, his head shaking in pretentious sorrow. He stared at the dead man who'd been placed on his left side, with his back facing the trunk lid. Eyes drooping, Gus puffed out his lower lip.

He blew a ball of smoke into the trunk. "I hate this part of my job. I really do. But as they say... shit happens. At least he's in a better place now." He turned toward Jesse, Rubin and Felipe. "You know what to do, boys."

Jesse and Rubin transferred the corpse from the trunk to the wheelbarrow. The dead man's clothes had once been a vibrant blue. But now, it was sodden and smeared with dirt and blood. The bullet hole Jesse had drilled into his skull was more or less like a third eye. It glistened with blood. His eyes were agape. Lifeless and cold, they seemed to settle on Gus.

● ● ●

"You'd think by now I'd have learned to use a body bag," Gus said, making a mental note to step up his game next time. "Jesus Christ! What a Goddamn mess!"

He trotted behind Felipe as he single-handedly pushed the wheelbarrow toward the large shed. Rubin and Jesse were on either side of the wheelbarrow, walking briskly to catch up.

They arrived at the incinerator shed, and Gus stood in the threshold, watching Felipe, Rubin and Jesse maneuver Mitch's body into the incinerator. The men stepped back, watching the body burn to ash. Gus nodded with accomplishment.

He tossed his cigarette to the ground. "Nice work, gentlemen. Nice work! I guess this is the part where I pay you for your hard work and dedication?" He searched his pockets. "Felipe, this is the second time you've done this for me. You put your job on the line just to make a few extra bucks. Let me repay you the very best way I know how. Turn around for a moment, it's a surprise."

Unsuspecting and eagerly anticipating, Felipe turned around, leaving his back vulnerable. Gus' fingers locked around a gun tucked into his waistline. He whipped it out and fired a bullet into the back of Felipe's head. Felipe met the floor with a heavy thud.

"Grab the keys from his pocket and throw him in there," Gus ordered.

Jesse and Rubin emptied Felipe's pockets.

Gus gave a second thought. "Ya know what? We might need that uniform. Strip him before you toss him in."

Forcing Felipe's lifeless body out of his uniform, Jesse and Rubin tossed him into the incinerator. Gus removed his ball cap—it had been crowning him ever since he stepped out during the early hours of the day—revealing a large scar running along his forehead.

• • •

A wave of fresh air whipped the scar, bringing his attention to it. And against his will, he remembered a certain night, years ago. The memory the scar triggered was just as ugly as the scar itself. He could vividly remember the slashing sound as a blade swung at him, finding flesh.

He lit another cigarette.

***

Ecstatic moans and whimpers flooded David's hotel room. And in between the sounds was the creaking and squeaking of the bed underneath him. He lay flat on his back, stripped of all clothing, and an equally nude woman—the redhead from the bar—impaled herself on his cock. She sat facing him, her breasts jiggling as she rode him hard and fast. She threw back her head in sheer pleasure, whimpering and cursing.

Her pussy sloshed with every slam, and a shrill cry tore through her lips every now and then. David ogled her, intoxicated by her soft moans and the glitter of pleasure in her eyes. He knew from her thickening voice that she was on the brink of orgasm. He was too—and he would shoot loads of cum inside of her until she overflowed. Hell, the sulky redhead was just as good in bed as she'd advertised.

His ringing cellphone on the nightstand by the left side of the bed caused him to halt. He clenched his teeth, hating the bad timing.

"Fuck!" He snatched the phone from the wooden surface and swiped across the screen to answer the call. "This better be good!"

"Tell your cock-sucking boss that his piece of shit limo will be parked exactly where he saw it last," a curt masculine voice rang through the phone speaker. "I no longer require its services."

The line went dead before David could say another word to the man who'd hijacked the limo. He stared gravely at the phone seconds after the call had ended. His cock deflated and he pulled out of the redhead, simultaneously shoving her off him.

The redhead rose from the bed, her eyes round with concern. "What's the matter?"

David returned the phone to the nightstand and swung his legs over the edge of the bed. Perched there, he grabbed his clothes which had been heaped on one side of the bed. The redhead stood watching him as he hastily dressed up.

"You can stay here or leave," he said, barely glancing in her direction, "but I need to go."

"Can I come with you?" She tentatively picked up her clothes.

"No! Ya know what? Just get dressed and get outta here." Now completely clad, David patted the front pockets of his pants, feeling for his wallet. Finding it, he pulled out some dollar notes and tossed them her way. "Take a cab home. Please, do yourself a favor."

"You rich bastards are all the same!" The redhead scrambled to get dressed.

She glowered at David, but it all was inconsequential to him. He picked up his phone again and put a call through to Jim Powers. He stood up, pacing the room as he waited for Jim to pick up. The first thing he heard when Jim answered the phone was a snort—inarguably the sound of him snorting a line of cocaine in the comforts of his luxurious estate.

"You're a real piece of shit," Jim said. "Ya know that?"

David was overwrought with confusion. "He just called! The guy who stole the limo!"

• • •

Not wanting the redhead to eavesdrop, David turned a corner and lowered his voice as he spoke on, "It sounds like he's gonna return it tonight. If we get there in time—"

"Whoa," Jim said, "whoa, whoa! Slow down there, chompy. Don't cum in your pants, for fuck's sake! I know this guy like the back of my goddamn hand! I have that son-of-a-bitch right where I want him."

"What do you mean?" David asked. "You know who stole the car?"

Jim exhaled noisily. "Yes, I know who stole the fucking car! Don't worry about it. Just do what I tell you and stop this goddamn paranoia or I swear, I will—"

David cut him off. "Hey, I realize you know what you're doing, but I'm just not following. I never should have gotten involved in this mess in the first place. I mean, one day I'm SVP of Marketing, the next day I'm tangled in a web of lies and deceit, money and murder. Peter out to get Paul, Paul out to get Mary, Mary out to get Peter. We're all just chasing our fucking tails over here. Nothing we do makes sense anymore. I don't think I can continue with this. Sorry, Jim, I want out."

"That's enough!" Jim barked an order.

A crash—a lot like the shattering of a glassware object—followed Jim's voice.

"You listen to me," Jim continued, "and you listen good, you whiny little bitch! You were there that night! It may not have been under the circumstances you were hoping for, but you were there and now you are part of this. That slut got exactly what she deserved. My issue with Gus may be completely unrelated, but you have been sucked into it by association. You have been more than generously compensated for everything and now you don't like it? Well, guess what? Too fucking bad! You ain't gettin' out now. I will tell you when this is over. You stab me in the back now and I swear to God, you will wish you were never born. Do I make myself clear?"

* * *

"Yes sir," David's voice squeezed through a lump in his throat.

"That's more like it." Jim hung up.

David slammed his fist into the wall, letting out all his pent up aggression on it. His eyes started to water, and with each passing second, it became more challenging to hold back the tears. They flowed down his cheeks like rivulets.

"You okay?" a soft voice asked. "What was that all about?"

David willed the tears to halt. He tilted his head toward the redhead whose presence he'd forgotten in his brief moment of vulnerability. She seemed genuinely concerned about him even though they were just random strangers.

He sniffled. "Nothing...really. Just work stuff. I'm under a lot of stress right now."

Another sniffle.

"Can you get room service to send up some bourbon?" he asked. "Makers Mark, if they have it. Tell them to charge it to the room."

"Uhhh, sure." Wide-eyed, she kept exploring him. "So we're staying, right?"

"For now."

CHAPTER SEVEN

Stephanie sat groggily with Rex by her side. She'd barely had any shut-eye all through the night; she felt more spent than she'd been her whole life. Brilliant rays of sunshine peeked through the blinds across from her, glaring at her. She turned away, feasting her eyes on her hands which she neatly arranged on her thighs. Without a moment's notice, she burst into tears, grabbed a tissue from the desk in front of her, and blotted her eyes. The puffiness of her eyes was enough evidence that she'd spent the whole night crying.

It was hard to believe Mitch was really gone. It all seemed like a dream. But there was no snapping out of this dream. Maybe if she hadn't gotten involved with the dog, then she wouldn't be here.

Rex uttered a low howl beside her, but she made no attempt to look at him. The damned creature was the reason she'd ended up in this state. She reached for a cup of coffee in front of her and took a sip. It had been sitting there long enough to grow cold, but prior to now she'd been unable to even acknowledge it.

"Can I get you some more coffee?" Officer Hansen of the Beverly Hills Police Department stepped into the office. He was the same officer who'd found her right after Mitch was murdered.

"Oh, uh...no, thank you. Have anymore Kleenex?" She blew her nose into the tissue.

"Coming right up," Hansen said. "Detective Palmer will be in shortly."

• • •

Stephanie acknowledged the statement with a nod, and Hansen disappeared to fetch the requested item. She drank the last of the coffee and set down the cup. The opening and closing of the door behind her and the shuffling of feet announced Detective Palmer's presence. He strode into her line of vision. The shadow of a smile lingered on his face, as though he and Stephanie were old acquaintances. For a cop, he seemed to have a bubbly personality. He was young—maybe a few years older than Mitch. Stephanie's thoughts settled on Mitch again. She remembered his eyes when he hit the ground. They'd been agape. The sight of lifeless eyes was a nightmare that would haunt her forever. They seemed to point at her, to pin her down with a burden of guilt.

Oblivious to her inner turmoil, Palmer set down a cup of coffee and hung his coat on a coat rack. Stephanie's eyes zeroed in on the gun glistening in its holster. She winced. It brought back memories of the previous evening.

"Can you please put that away?" she freaked out. "The gun! Please!"

"Hey," Palmer held out his hands to calm her, "hey...it's okay. I'll take it off. How about I put it in this drawer, huh?"

He placed the weapon in a drawer, took a seat across from her, and extended his hand in an introduction. "I'm Detective Palmer. And you are?"

"Stephanie." She shook hands with him.

"It's a pleasure to meet you, Stephanie. I'm really sorry we have to meet under these conditions, but you can rest assured, we will do whatever we can to bring these guys to justice." He flashed Rex a stiff smile. "I see you brought your dog?"

Stephanie huffed. "I'm not talking to him right now. This is all his fault!"

She folded her arms across her chest.

Palmer chuckled. "Now how can this possibly be his fault?"

• • •

A knock on the door disrupted their conversation, forcing Stephanie's response to die on her lips. Rex protectively leapt to his feet, his eyes fixated on the door. Detective Palmer signaled for Officer Hansen to enter. Hansen walked into the office, bearing a box of tissues. He handed it over to Stephanie.

"I took these from Cathy's desk," he said.

Stephanie figured out Cathy was a female officer.

"—so I hope you appreciate it!" Hansen flashed her a flirtatious smile.

"I do, thank you." Stephanie smiled weakly.

Palmer only resumed his conversation with Stephanie after Hansen had left. "Stephanie, I understand you feel as though you can't talk. The first thing a bad guy will tell you is not to go to the cops. Not to say anything to anyone. They'll usually threaten to harm you or your family as a means to keep you quiet, which I'm guessing is the case here. Am I right?"

Stephanie nodded. The movement of her head was barely noticeable, but Palmer's intent gaze caught it anyway.

"Don't let that deter you from doing the right thing," he urged. "Tell me everything that happened last night."

Stephanie glanced over her shoulder. Hansen had shut the door on his way out, but her unease remained.

"Don't worry. Nobody's listening, just me." Palmer produced a note-pad and a pen from the top drawer of his desk. He flipped to a blank page and bookmarked it with the pen.

Stephanie mustered up the courage to speak. "Mitch and I had just parked our car and were walking to dinner."

"What street were you on?" he asked.

Stephanie tried to recollect the details, but they eluded her. She gave up after a few attempts. "Gosh, I can't remember right now. My mind is kinda foggy. I'm sorry."

• • •

"No, no, that's okay. Just tell me what you remember. My apologies for interrupting you. Go on."

"Okay, we were walking and this homeless guy stopped us and begged us for help."

The detective jotted down some notes. "Okay."

"Well, that's where he—" She pointed to Rex, "comes into play."

Palmer's brows furrowed as he struggled to understand the statement.

"The homeless guy showed us a picture of the dog and asked if we'd help locate him," Stephanie explained, noting Palmer's confusion. "Apparently, the dog was stolen from him the night before."

She paused, searching his face for an expression. He seemed to be following along just fine.

"Hmmm," he said. "Okay, go on."

"Well, I felt bad for him and wanted to help. Mitch just wanted to keep going." Stephanie erupted into tears. "I'm so stupid! I never listen to anyone. I always have to be this righteous person and now he's gone. He's dead and it's all my fault!"

"Hey, hey, it's not your fault, okay? You need to stop that train of thought right now or we'll never catch these guys. Tell me what happened next."

Stephanie stayed silent as though Palmer had never spoken. Sure, it was easy for a stranger to say none of this was her fault. And it'd be even easier for them to expect her to snap out of her grief and get on with life as though a devastating explosion had not shaken her to the core.

"I really don't mean to be insensitive," Palmer said, "but I want these guys off the street as badly as you do. I need you to keep talking, please."

PAWN

Stephanie pulled herself together. "We told him—" She shrugged. "Well, I told him that we'd help find his dog. I relayed to him that I was a pit bull lover who understood what he was going through."

"So...you were being a caring, sensitive, compassionate person. I don't see anything wrong with that."

"At that point, a police car came zooming around the corner and the homeless guy bolted like there was no tomorrow. It was weird. He appeared ailing until he saw those lights and boom! He was off."

"It's amazing what adrenaline can do for people."

"When Officer Hansen started chasing after him, we decided to get the hell out of dodge. I suggested that we take a shortcut through the alley, which we did. That's when we bumped into this guy who was walking Rex. We recognized Rex as the dog from the picture."

Palmer glanced at Rex. "Now, are you positive it's the exact same dog? I mean, pit bulls can look similar, right?"

"Uhhh...yeah," Stephanie said. She followed Palmer's gaze. There was no mistaking this was the exact same dog on the picture the homeless man had been parading the streets with. "I guess. I'm pretty sure, though."

"At this point it's not going to change the outcome," Palmer said. "But if it is the same dog, it sounds like we have a scam artist working the streets."

Stephanie jolted with excitement as a slice of memory fell into place like a jigsaw puzzle. "No, wait! I remember now. The homeless guy told us the dog's name was Rex. The guy in the alley also said his name was Rex. That's how we knew it was the same dog!"

"There you go!" Palmer said. "Now you're starting to put the puzzle together. Good job! Okay, so you started talking to this guy?"

Stephanie's face took on a more wistful look. "Yeah, we started talking and within seconds we had company in the form of two other guys, one of which had a gun aimed at Mitch. The other guy grabbed me and covered my mouth."

"And what happened with the guy who was walking the dog?" Palmer asked.

"That's the thing. They were all connected. It was a set-up. He's the one who ordered for Mitch to be executed."

"Did they harm you at all?"

"No." Stephanie gave Palmer's question a second thought. "Well...mentally, yes! He knew my name, which really freaked me out. Makes me think he's been watching me or something."

"It's not hard to find someone's name," Palmer stated. "The question is, why you guys? It could have been random, but the fact that he pointed out that he knows your name tells me that it was possibly planned. You know anyone who wants to harm you?"

"No!" Stephanie blurted out, appalled that anyone would want to harm her.

"What about Mitch?" Palmer asked. "Can you think of any reason someone would want to harm him?"

"I barely knew the guy" Stephanie replied. "It was our first actual date."

Detective Palmer jotted this down.

"What did they do with Mitch's body?" Palmer asked.

"They carried him over to a black limousine and shoved him into the trunk," Stephanie said. "After that, I don't know. I tried to make out the license place, but I couldn't. I think the first letter was 'J' though."

She tried to remember the second letter. She shook her head; it was no use trying to. Her vision of it had been a blur.

• • •

Palmer jotted down some more notes. "How did you end up with the dog?"

"He just handed me the leash and they drove off," Stephanie said.

Palmer put the pieces together. "And that's when Officer Hansen found you?"

"Correct," Stephanie said.

Palmer reviewed his notes. Done, he looked up at Stephanie. "Very good. You remember quite a lot for someone who just went through such a traumatic experience."

"How can I forget?" Stephanie asked. The previous night's experience seared her heart like a hot iron branding. It would be forever fresh in her memory.

"I'm going to have you meet with Jenine our sketch artist," Palmer said. "She will ask you to describe the three men. Can you do that for her?"

"Yeah," Stephanie said without a second thought. "I think so."

Sure, it'd been dark, but she'd been able to make out their faces, particularly that of the ringleader. He had a face she would never forget in a hurry. Even when he'd switched roles from a friendly stranger to a cold-hearted murderer, the look in his eyes had stayed warm and amicable as though the whole episode was a joke.

Palmer's voice cut through her retrospection. "Okay. Here's my card."

He held out a business card toward her. She plucked it out of his hold, gave it a once-over, then placed it in her purse.

"Call me anytime, day or night. That's my cell." He stood up and gestured for her to follow suit. "Follow me. You can leave the pooch in here for a while. He'll be okay."

* * *

He led her out of the office and into the main hall. It bustled with police officers who were all engrossed in their individual duties. He approached a lady digging through a file cabinet. Stephanie followed him closely.

"Jenine, this is Stephanie," Palmer said. "She is going to describe three suspects for you."

Jenine gripped Stephanie's hand in a firm handshake. "Hi, Stephanie. I'll be with you in just a minute. Why don't you take a seat on that stool over there—" She gestured to a stool by her desk, "and I'll join you as soon as I'm done here."

Stephanie sat down on the stool. A sketch pad on the desk caught her eye and she stared at it for a second too long.

"I'll be in touch, kiddo," Palmer said to Stephanie. "Call me anytime."

Stephanie looked up at him. "Thank you."

Raising his hand in departure, he walked away.

CHAPTER EIGHT

Melissa lay sprawled out on her bed, face down and naked. Her tousled hair snaked around her like tentacles, reaching sideways to touch the edges of the bed. A wine bottle, wine glass and bottle of pills conspicuously loomed in the background. The loud crash of a heavy object breaching her bedroom window yanked her into consciousness.

She woke up to a pacing heart. "Jesus Christ! What the fuck was that?"

She stood up from the bed and a flash of pain erupted in her forehead. She clutched her head, searching for her bearings. Just as she flung on her bathrobe, she caught sight of her shattered window and the shards of glass scattered across the floor. A fist-sized rock sat in the midst of the glass.

Melissa slid her feet into her flip-flops beside the bed and stealthily made her way through the glass to pick up the rock. She looked out through the window to find whoever had hurled the rock at her. Her cautious eyes scanned the crowd walking down both sides of the street as typical of a workday morning. There was nothing out of the ordinary. With a sigh of resignation, she looked down at the rock. She began to toss it back out the window, but in mid-action, she found a handwritten message on the other side of it. It was scribbled in black ink.

The message was a curt two-word sentence. *Call Chris.*

She looked over to the still-made bed, and then it struck her that Chris probably hadn't returned home the previous night. She'd been too hammered to stay up waiting for him, especially after finding out he was well on his way to cheating on her. Staring one last time at the rock, she placed it on her nightstand.

She stormed out of the room and burst through the hallway, frantic to find a sign of life. "Chris?"

She marched to the twins' room and poked her head inside. "Kids?"

An unnerving silence greeted her. The house suddenly seemed more gigantic than usual, and her tensed voice bounced off the walls.

In a state of panic, she darted downstairs, taking the steps two at a time. "Alex? Joshua?"

She broke into a run as she headed for the family room. Animated voices streaked into her ears from the television. On arrival, she found Joshua and Alex calmly sitting in front of the television, glued to a cartoon.

She sighed with relief. "You guys scared me!"

The kids were too engrossed in the cartoon and didn't spare a moment to acknowledge her.

"Hey!" she called, pissed off.

Still nothing.

Melissa strode to the back of the TV and yanked the power cord from the wall. The TV died, and the twins finally looked in her direction.

"Hey!" they both said in a mild protest.

"We were watching that!" Alex whined, his tiny and adorable voice almost resembling that of the cartoon he'd been watching.

Melissa stood akimbo. "Where's daddy?"

Alex fumed. "I don't know!"

Melissa stared from Alex to Joshua. Joshua looked away from her and rested his head on the armrest of the chair. Melissa cooled her engines, plugged the TV back in, and marched to the kitchen.

She paced the breadth of the kitchen, her thoughts occasionally drifting to the message on the rock. She strode to the telephone and dialed Chris' number. Even without the anonymous message on the rock, she would have contacted him anyway. That was pretty much what any woman would do when she woke up to the realization that her husband had not returned home throughout the night.

Had he perhaps decided to spend the night at his mother's? It didn't seem like it. When he'd called during the night, he'd been on his way home. She'd deduced that from the familiar music spilling out of the car's stereo. The thought that something might have gone wrong occurred to her, but she didn't dwell on it.

She pressed the phone to her right ear, sucking in deep breaths to stay calm as she waited for him to pick up.

Chris answered the call. "Melissa?"

"Where the hell are you?" Melissa asked.

"Well, honey, it's the strangest thing." Chris' voice was low and rather incoherent. Melissa had to strain her ears to hear him.

Her worry morphed into rage. "No! No, Chris. I'm sick and tired of your excuses! It's always the strangest thing. I know you're back on that shit! I'm not stupid. Strange packages arriving at your parents' house, money disappearing from our checking account and nothing to show for it. Was rehab just a joke to you? It's time to grow the fuck up!"

Without giving him a chance to speak, she kept berating him. "Ya know what? I don't care where you are anymore. Just stay the fuck out of my house! As far as I'm concerned, this marriage is over!"

She slammed the receiver into the cradle. She stood still, still gripping the phone. Her whole body trembled with rage and her eyes started to blur with tears. She squeezed her eyes shut, and when she popped them back open, the tears were gone. Chris wasn't worth a single tear.

***

"You done?" Jim asked, gluing a phone to Chris' right ear. His other hand clutched a knife which he pressed against Chris' throat. He held the knife just below Chris' bobbing Adam's apple.

Chris sniffled, tears streaming down his cheeks. "Yes."

Severely beaten, he sat between David and Jim in a limo. His hands were bound tightly behind his back; he could barely even move a muscle.

Jim shifted on the seat as he detached the phone from David's ear and tossed it sideways. He chuckled. "You didn't even have to follow the script! I guess having a bitch flap her gums can sometimes work out in a guy's favor, huh? What'd she say?"

"She told me not to come home," Chris forced out the words even as they weighed heavily on his swollen lip.

Jim roared with laughter. He shook his head disappointingly, still holding the knife to Chris' throat. The knife scraped his skin, drawing blood. David sat in paranoid discomfort, squirming. His wish to be someplace else was apparent from the detached look on his face.

"What kind of a pussy-whipped little prick are ya, eh? The day any broad said that to me would be the last time she said anything at all! First of all, you're gonna leave this package with us." Jim kicked a conspicuous brown box that'd been lying in front of them. "The amount of debt you're in, you'll never pay me back. This should be enough to keep you alive though." He snickered. "For now."

Stripped of every ounce of dignity, Chris lost composure. "Please! Just let me go. I'll get you the money, I swear! I'll do whatever you say. Don't bring my wife and kids into this. They don't deserve it."

Without warning, Jim leaned back and slammed the heel of his shoe into Chris' jaw. Knocked out, Chris fell face down into David's lap.

Jim grabbed him by the hair and spoke directly into his ear, "Excuse me, but did you say *your* kids? Just because your wife gave birth to them doesn't make them your kids, jackass! And just because that slut made a good sperm depository doesn't make me a father, now does it?"

Chris lay comatose.

Still, Jim went on, "What's the matter? You don't like the fact that I fucked your wife and you're paying to raise the kids? Perhaps you wonder why she never said anything to you...never went to the cops? What the hell am I explaining this to you for? You'll never remember this conversation just like she'll never remember that night."

David jolted in his seat as he peered out of the rear window. "Shit!"

Jim followed David's gaze and sighted a police car approaching from a distance. He calmly tossed his coat over the brown box on the floor. He crossed his legs, waiting for a police officer to approach them. He knew it was sure to happen.

As expected, the police car pulled up behind the limo and a nosy officer advanced to the window. He knocked, squinting to see through the glass.

● ● ●

Jim rolled down the window. "Good morning, officer." He glanced down at the officer's name tag. "Hansen. You must be new?"

Officer Hansen peered into the vehicle through the open window. He stared wearily at Chris who still lay face-down on David's lap. Jim nonchalantly looked over to Chris and then back up at Officer Hansen.

"This kid, I tell ya! I turn my back for one second and he's out for a night of binge drinking. We just found him passed out on the pavement. We're trying to sober him up." Jim let out a soft sigh, feigning frustration. He gently slapped Chris' face. "Wake up, son. It's time to take you home."

"What happened to his face?" Hansen asked, staring a hole through Chris.

"One of his buddies called me," Jim narrated, "said he was involved in a bar-room-brawl. That's when I came looking for him and found him here. He'll be fine. Happens all the time."

The officer didn't seem convinced. "Can I see some I.D., please?"

"Of course!" Jim slid a wallet out of his pocket. He retrieved his driver's license and handed it to Officer Hansen.

A smile lit up Hansen's face as he perused the I.D. "Ahhh, the famous Jim Powers, huh? I've heard a lot of great things about you at the station!"

He flashed Jim a 'keep-it-on-the-down-low' wink.

"I don't know about famous," Jim said, "but I do know that everyone at the station is quite fond of me. We work as a team to keep the streets clean. I help them, they help me. It's a beautiful thing."

"Hey Jim," Hansen said, "do me a favor, would ya? Go ahead and open the trunk for me. I know you have nothing to hide, just following protocol."

"Officer Hansen—"

"You can call me Bob."

"Bob, you don't need to see what's in the trunk. What you want to see is right here inside the limo! Come on in, please."

Officer Hansen swept his eyes around the road, making sure the coast was clear, then he hopped into the limo. Without trepidation, he closed the door behind him.

Jim set a briefcase down on his lap and flipped open the latches, arrogantly revealing its contents to Officer Hansen. Stacks of crisp, one-hundred-dollar-bill bundles lined the briefcase.

"Now I would strongly advise against bribery," Hansen said, but the words didn't seem to come from him. They'd come off as robotic, as though he'd been programmed to say that whenever he was met with a generous act. "That would be wrong!"

"Oh," Jim said in a gratuitous voice, "very wrong! And it's such an inconvenience when I accidentally drop a few bundles of cash on the floor...like this."

Jim ostentatiously showered the limo floor with cash.

"Money just seems to slip through my hands!" Jim shook his head with a mocking sense of naivety.

Chris stirred, slowly regaining consciousness.

"Hey," David said, "it looks like the kid is starting to sober up now. Maybe we should get going?"

Jim shot David a cold stare that could easily pass for a glare. "Relax, will ya?"

Hansen pointed to David. "Who's he?"

"That's David,"Jim said. "He works for me."

"Ahhh. Just so you guys know, we're—" Hansen signaled quotation marks with both hands. "'—supposed to be' looking for a limo just like this. There was a murder and the victim was stuffed into the trunk. I'm sure it wasn't this one. Just want you fellas to know."

He flashed Jim a patronizing wink.

"Thanks for the heads up," Jim said, "but just so *you* know, we have nothing to do with it. I know who did, though."

"Oh?" Hansen arched his brows—a subtle probing for more information, Jim supposed.

"Don't worry," Jim said, "he'll serve a sentence far worse than the judicial system could ever dish out. Like I said, I'm here to help you fine people keep our streets clean. David, hand me that black bag, will ya?"

David complied.

Jim graciously handed over the black bag to Hansen. "Place the cash in here. Do yourself a favor and don't deposit it. Just spend it little bits at a time so not to raise flags with the I.R.S. Got it?"

"Got it!" Hansen said.

"Those bastards fucked me over more than once," Jim said, "and this is my little way of getting even with them."

Lowering himself to a squat, Hansen stuffed the bag like a kid in a candy shop. "You gentlemen have yourselves a splendid day!"

"You do the same, Bob," Jim said.

Hansen waved at Jim just before exiting the vehicle and closing the door behind him.

Jim growled his frustration at David. "You really need to get a grip. If I tell you I have everything under control, it means I have everything under control."

David nodded sheepishly.

Jim stole a glance at Chris. "Hey, kid! Can you hear me?"

* * *

If this was a sobriety test, Chris would spend the night in jail.

"Mmmm," Chris moaned, shifting into a more comfortable position. "Melissa, is that you? Where am I?"

"Un-fucking-believable!" Jim said. "The kid's supposed to be some martial arts wiz and he can't even recover from a swift kick to the chops!"

He turned toward David. "I have something to take care of. Keep an eye on him and don't let him out of your sight! When he comes around, give me a call on my cell. I have a few matters to discuss with him. You got that?"

"Yeah, got it."

"Don't worry so much. This will all be over real soon and you can get back to your boring, non-existent life. You're doing good. Just don't let me down."

Jim exited the limo. The glare of sunlight was harsh against his eyes. He squinted, blocking out the rays of sunlight as he jaywalked across the street to his parked Lamborghini. He ducked behind the wheel and started the engine.

• • •

CHAPTER NINE

Melissa couldn't help the quiver in her throat as she hugged and kissed her twin boys. Across from her stood her parents—Henry and Cynthia—with two junior suitcases standing beside them in the entryway. Although Joshua and Alex hadn't left yet, she missed them already. But sending them away for a few days was the best decision she could come up with. She'd phoned her parents an hour or so ago and they'd reached the decision together. With Chris away and without a source of income, she couldn't handle having the boys around.

Added to that was the possibility of Chris coming around. A fight might ensue and the last thing she wanted was staining her kids' childhood with such ugly memories.

"Now you boys be good for grandma and grandpa," Melissa said, "okay?"

"Are they gonna buy us candy?" Joshua asked. His eyes were aglow with excitement.

The look in Alex's eyes was no different. "And toys?"

"Oh boy, Cynthia! What are we getting ourselves into?" Henry had spoken into Cynthia's ears, but Melissa caught the words anyway.

"Stop it, Henry!" Cynthia elbowed him. "They're old enough to understand."

Melissa let out a humbling sigh. "Thank you so very much for taking them for a few days. You guys are lifesavers!"

* * *

"It's the least we can do, sweetheart," Cynthia said. "Take all the time you need to get everything under control. Your father and I understand."

"I'm sure Chris will shape up, honey," Henry said.

Melissa sighed. A part of her wanted that too—raising the boys alone would weigh her down. But a greater part of her wanted him gone. Lately, Chris had become too contemptible for her liking. She'd not exactly married a 'Prince Charming', but life with him had been quite tolerable, until lately. Maybe shutting him out was the only way she could get her life back together. She just didn't see a future with a man like Chris.

"I don't know, dad," Melissa said. "I really think we're through this time. I can't do this forever. Anyway, I need a few days to think about everything and look for a job. It's a bit hard with two four-year-olds and I can't afford daycare right now."

"Eh, forget about it!" Henry said, staring at the kids in admiration. "They'll be fine with us. We'll call you if we have any trouble."

Melissa stepped forward and snaked her arms around her parents in a heartfelt embrace. "I love you guys."

She pulled out of the hug and turned toward her kids, crouching so their gazes were level. All smiles, she ruffled Alex's hair and squeezed Joshua's cheeks. "I love you guys too!"

Joshua fell into her arms, wrapping his tiny arms tight around her. Alex joined him, and they held still for what seemed like forever.

"Come on, kids," Cynthia said. "Let's go grab a hamburger!"

Alex and Joshua sprang out of the hug. "Yay!"

Luggage in tow, Henry and Cynthia escorted the twins out the front door.

● ● ●

"Bye, guys! Be good." Melissa waved the twins goodbye as they jumped into the back seat of Henry's car.

She watched Henry heave the luggage into the trunk and join the others in the car. He pulled out of the driveway, and the kids gave Melissa an animated wave. She waved back, watching until the car rounded a corner and disappeared out of sight.

With a slight reservation, she shut the door and headed up the stairs to the home office. Once there, she slid into the desk chair and logged onto Chris' internet account.

Eagerly anticipating, she clicked on a new email from Satin_Damsel95. *Hey, Rob. Sorry it's taken me so long to respond. Something terrible happened and I'm really not myself right now. I'll be okay...just a bit traumatized. I wish you were here with me. I'm scared and lonely. Anyway, about your sister, I work for a finance company as a loan processor. As fate would have it, we're swamped and could use some help. Send me her resumé and I'll see what I can do. Thanks for being such a great friend. Talk to ya soon.*

Melissa's words appeared on the monitor. *Oh, wow! I had no idea. I'm so sorry! You are way too beautiful to feel so blue! Please let me know what I can do to comfort you. I wish I could come over there and hold you, but I can't. I hope you understand. I'll sign on again this evening. Why don't you join me so we can chat? Everything will be okay...I promise. Oh, and about the job... you are a doll! Attached is my sister's resumé. Love, Rob.*

She attached a copy of her resumé and clicked 'send.' A jittery feeling overwhelmed her and she leaned back in the chair, swiveling left and right as she awaited the girl's response.

● ● ●

CHAPTER TEN

Empty and lavish, Jim slipped in through the gigantic double doors of a church. He was dressed in his signature style—a tailored black suit with a heavenly white shirt peeking out underneath. He took a deep breath, looked around, and spotted Father Tim enjoying water from a drinking fountain. The man was eleven years Jim's senior. It had been years since Jim had last seen him, but the old man was just the same. Age seemed to be going easy on him—well it seemed to be considerate with the two men.

Jim halted only a few steps away from the doorway. Father Tim was yet to learn of his presence. He could return unnoticed. He didn't have to push through with his reason for visiting the church. He rebuked his uncertainty. Jim Powers had never been one to chicken out. The past five years had been hell, and with every night came a nightmare—a recollection of his grievous sin. And somehow he believed emptying himself to the Lord would bring some measure of relief. It was a practice he'd always relied on, back in the days when life was a walk in the park.

And it had never failed him.

With his resolve now reinforced, Jim cracked a weak smile as he started toward Father Tim. "Good afternoon, Father."

Father Tim took his last sip and looked up at Jim. He lit up like a Christmas tree as he welcomed an estranged, yet familiar face.

"Well, look who's here!" Father Tim said in an Irish brogue. "Jimmy, me boy. What a pleasant surprise!"

Being in Father Tim's presence invoked an otherwise unattainable calmness in Jim. He'd been counting on that. "You're not gonna drop dead from shock, are ya?"

Father Tim laughed. "Oh, no! It'll take a lot more than seeing you back in the Church to give me a coronary! How the heck are ya, kid? I haven't seen you since your father passed. God bless his soul."

"Yeah," Jim said. "I've been well. Just really busy with work. I still have the company. Business is good. You received my last donation, right?"

Father Tim beamed at him. "Oh, Jimmy! Your father would be very proud. That was an extremely generous donation and it will help many less fortunate people. I just about fell off my chair when I saw the check. It's too much."

"What? First we don't give enough, then we give too much. You're killing me!" He shared a laugh with Father Tim.

"It is your gift to share and you may do with it as you see fit. I do appreciate it." Father Tim cleared his throat. "What brings you here today, son?"

Jim grew restive. He shifted his weight to his left leg, and finding this new posture more comfortable, he chose to maintain it. But his fidgety spirit decided otherwise, making him unsure of how to stand or where to place his hands. Sticking his hands in his pants pockets seemed to alleviate his tenseness. But that was only for a moment. He didn't think it right to stand that way in front of a priest. He folded his arms, and even though he didn't feel right about this stance, he maintained it anyway. Sure, it seemed condescending to the priest, but that was all he could manage at the moment. He glanced down at his shoes, as though their luster were some sort of enchantment.

He sighed heavily. He knew the only way out of his restlessness was to open up to Father Tim. He was frantic to rid himself of the heavy burden pressing down on him. He lifted his head so his gaze was level with Father Tim's. The old man's gaze was warm and inviting, spurring him on.

"I need to talk, Father," he finally brought himself to utter the words. "Can you spare some time right now?"

"There is always time!" Father Tim said. "The sacrament of reconciliation is amongst our most important. Someone is in the confessional booth right now. Let's go into my office."

They proceeded down a long, sterile hallway leading to Father Tim's office. Rays of sunlight seeped in through the stained glass windows overhead, flooding the hallway with a golden glimmer. All through the walk, neither said a word to the other. Only the sounds of footsteps as the soles of their shoes slapped the floor could be heard.

Upon entering the office, Father Tim closed the door behind them. He gestured toward a round conference table. "Take a seat, son."

Jim plopped down on a chair and Father Tim took a seat opposite him.

"What seems to be troubling you?" Father Tim regarded him the way a father would a son.

Before Jim could answer, Father Tim covered his hand with his and looked him in the eye. The subtle gesture stirred up a warmth in Jim's chest.

"I remind you that everything we discuss here is strictly confidential," Father Tim spoke quietly, "no matter what its content. This is your opportunity to absolve yourself of sins and ask God for His forgiveness."

"Maybe I just wanted to discuss the SC/Notre Dame game?"

Jim's question broke the tension in the office, drawing out a laugh from the older man. He laughed too, but only for a moment. The tension returned, full force this time, hitting him squarely in the chest.

Distracted, he sighed again. "Oh, Father. I don't even know where to begin."

"Just start from the beginning," Father Tim urged. "I have all the time in the world."

"A lot of things have happened over the years. The Jim Powers everybody knew and loved is gone and I don't know where to find him." Jim tried to hold his composure, refraining from becoming overly emotional.

"Go on, son."

"As you know, my dad left me the company and a lot of money. I mean, a lot of money! I really loved my dad. He meant everything to me. I guess you can say I changed when he was savagely murdered."

Jim cringed at the memory of three unrecognizable men pummeling his elderly father in the dark of night. He could still remember the sound of rain pelting down on the desolate pavement, muffling his father's cries as the men pounded him from all angles. As a final blow, they'd smashed his head with a brick. A homeless man had been watching from a distance, wincing with every blow, unable to lift a finger in the old man's defense. He couldn't help but notice what appeared to be an unmarked police car within earshot of the crime scene. Strange, he thought. But he was more concerned about his safety.

"They wanted money from him," he continued. "He didn't have enough in his wallet. I lost a great deal of respect for society, the authorities, the legal system, the judicial system. Something snapped inside of me and I decided that I needed to take charge and restore order. If I wanted something, I had to go out and get it all on my own. I felt like I could depend on nobody. Not even God. All the digging around, the leads, it amounted to nothing. The authorities couldn't find the guys who killed my dad, so I took it upon myself to find them, which I did. It was at that point that I crossed over into a very dark place. The place that I find myself in now."

Jim's voice had begun to crack, and his throat had gone dry toward his last few words.

"Excuse me for just a moment," Father Tim said. "Let me get you some water."

He stood up, poured a glass of water from a pitcher, and slid it over to Jim.

Jim took a sip. "Thank you, Father."

"What happened when you found the men who were responsible?" Father Tim asked. "How did you know they weren't wrongly accused?"

"They tried to extort money from me after the dust settled," Jim explained, "and they knew how much I was worth. A few traceable phone calls, many sloppy mistakes. I knew exactly who the three guys were. I learned where each of them lived and decided to pay one of them a visit."

That was only six years ago.

"One night, I quietly entered the first guy's apartment. I'd been staking him out so I knew he was home asleep."

Dressed in black from head-to-toe and carrying a duffel bag, Jim had snuck into the man's apartment. The ambiance reeked of poverty and crime. He closed the door, careful not to make a sound. He crept toward the bedroom, and an animalistic snore grew louder with every step he took.

The thug lay face down, sound asleep in his dimly lit bedroom. Jim quietly set the duffel bag down, unzipped it slowly, and meticulously removed a baseball bat, a knife, a pair of gardening shears and some rope. He fixated his eyes on the thug, alert for any shift in his position.

• • •

Chin sticking out with an unfaltering resolve, Jim wielded the bat as he approached his prey with purpose. He peered at him with disgust, then whacked him in the back of the head.

"The first blow to his head had immobilized him. Kinda like when you clunk a rat's head on a hard surface before feeding it to a snake. It prevents the rat from biting the snake."

Father Tim shifted in his seat, his slackening face suggesting that he might be uncomfortable. "You struck him with the baseball bat?"

"I could have done it harder," Jim said, "but my goal wasn't to kill him. I wanted him to suffer for the rest of his life."

"God punishes people like him, Jim. That is a huge part of our faith. It's not our job to play God." Father Tim stayed silent for a moment, and then he popped a question. "What did you do with the knife, the shears and the rope?"

Jim was starting to have second thoughts about his conversation with the priest. "I don't know if I should tell you. Maybe this isn't such a good idea. You are going to think differently of me."

"Jim, let it go," Father Tim said. "If you don't, you will carry this very heavy cross with you for the rest of your life. Let's continue, please."

Jim took a deep breath. A reluctant sigh slipped across his thin lips as he slid back into his memories. "While the guy was knocked out from the blow, I stripped him down completely naked and tied him to the four bed posts. I then watched and waited for him to regain consciousness."

The thug had let out a throaty moan as he slowly reached consciousness. His eyes had fluttered, and then they'd narrowed open. Jim hovered over him, flashing him a sinister smirk as he ballistically struggled to break free.

'You fucking piece of shit!' the thug spat. 'Fight me like a real man, you fucking pussy! '

Jim sadistically looked him in the eye. Without a word, he cocked his head to the side.

'You don't have the fucking balls to kill me!' the thug dared.

Jim held on to his calmness. 'I don't plan to.'

'That's what I thought, bitch! Your sorry-ass old man deserved to die and you are next.' The thug spat in Jim's face. 'Cock-sucker!'

In response to the thug's ranting, Jim exposed his razor-sharp knife. He'd been holding it behind him all along. The thug's eyes bulged out of their sockets as his imminent end dawned on him. Once again, he struggled to beak free.

'Help!' he screamed. 'Hel—'

Before he could finish his word, Jim thrust the knife into his throat, twisting it with a quarter turn. Still, the thug tried to scream, but instead of words, flashes of hot breath burst out of his mouth.

'Help,' he mouthed.

Jim had plunged the knife deeper into his larynx. 'You are going to pay dearly for what you fuck-heads did to my father. You'd be goddamn lucky if I kill you. That would be the easy way out.'

Perhaps if the thug could, he'd beg for mercy at this point. But with his larynx completely destroyed, he would never be able to utter another sound again. The thought of cutting off the man's genitals crossed Jim's mind, but he decided against it—he wanted him to have insatiable urges.

Knife firmly in his grasp, he surgically peeled off the skin from the thug's face. Frantic for an escape, the thug thrashed his head around with his residual energy. Blood splattered on the wall as he did so.

Jim tossed the knife to the ground and grabbed the baseball bat. He thrust the handle into the thug's mouth, shattering his teeth. The thug spewed out blood and tooth fragments. Jim replaced the baseball bat with the gardening shears. He snipped off the fingers and toes of the thug. With each cut, blood spurted from the severed digits. Now with all of the thug's fingers and toes completely lopped off below the joint, suicide would be unachievable.

Jim strolled to the bathroom and ripped the mirror off the medicine cabinet. Mirror in hand, he returned to the thug and held it an inch away from his face. The thug jerked his face sideways, refusing to stare into the mirror. He kept struggling to break free, but he stood no chance against the ropes restraining him. Jim had wound the sturdy ropes against his wrists and ankles multiple times before tying them in compact knots.

He tossed the mirror aside and grabbed the bat again. This time, he went for the thug's knees, striking them so hard he could hear the snapping of bones. He looked down at the thug, his heart overflowing with satisfaction. No surgery could ever repair the damage he'd done.

He picked up a cellphone from a nearby nightstand, and dialed one of the thug's accomplices. The second thug picked up as though he'd waited for the phone call all his life.

"Dude, why the fuck you calling so late?" the second thug snapped.

"This ain't who you think it is," Jim said in a flat tone, "but I suggest that you get to his apartment ASAP. He could use your help."

He hung up and tossed the phone onto the bed. He rifled the nightstand drawers in search of some writing materials. A torn envelope wasn't exactly what he'd had in mind, but it would serve the purpose. Finding a pen, he scribbled a note on the back of the envelope. Done, he'd flung off the pen, sending it rolling to the other side of the room. He'd held the envelope above the bed and had impaled it into the wall with the knife.

• • •

Father Tim covered his mouth with his left hand. His face had turned pale in the course of Jim's narration.

"You okay?" Jim asked.

"I'm fine. I just need a sip of your water." He grabbed the glass of water from the table and took a sip. "That's better."

The two men grew silent. Jim gazed at Father Tim, anticipating his next words. But it seemed the priest was waiting for him to break the silence.

Father Tim spoke after forever. "What did the note say?"

Jim looked down at the table, and when he looked up at Father Tim, his eyes were menacing. "You're next!"

Father Tim gasped. "Oh, my! What happened when his friend found him?"

"I left the scene at that point," Jim said. "But not before installing cameras."

Soon after Jim had departed from the thug's apartment, the other two thugs—one of which was Gus, the ringleader—had proceeded into the bedroom. Their strides were slow as though they suspected whoever had been there was still around. They surveyed the blood-curdling scene, wincing at their friend's mangled body in horror. They watched him in his sorry state, his unrecognizable face painted red with his own blood.

He opened his mouth to speak, but his words were a tortuous wheeze. Blood spurted from his hands and feet, forming thick puddles on the floor around him.

Gus swallowed hard. 'Put a bullet in his brain.'

Gun in hand, the second thug had approached his mangled friend with trepidation. He'd finally mustered up the courage, shooting him between the eyes at close range.

"They then drove the body to a pet cemetery," Jim said. "I never really left. I sat waiting in my car parked a distance away from the apartment. I watched them transfer their friend's corpse into the trunk of their car, and then I followed them from a distance. They threw him into an incinerator to dispose of him. He would never be seen or heard from again, and quite frankly, nobody even cared enough to go looking."

"That is quite a story, Jim," Father Tim said.

"The accomplice who was ordered to shoot him got into an altercation with Gus," Jim went on with his story as though Father Tim had not uttered a word. "Unknown to Gus, the thug had yanked out the knife I'd stabbed into the wall. He swung wildly at Gus, slashing open his forehead. Had the knife slit his throat he'd be a goner today. For his sake...good thing he moved out of the way. The thug tried to ditch the scene, but Gus pulled out a gun, firing a fatal round into his back. With the help of an insider, they threw his body into the incinerator as well. A lot of evidential blood was left at both scenes, but I paid off the cops to stay out of it. I told them to let me handle it and for the right price, they all turned a blind eye."

"Crooked cops in our city? I'd never have guessed." Father Tim cleared his throat. "Now that you have confessed your sins, Jim, it's important for you to repent and let God know you are truly sorry and that you need his forgiveness. Are you truly sorry for what you've done?"

Jim snickered. "For that? Hell no! For what I'm about to tell you next...yes."

Father Tim clutched his chest as though a sword had just sliced through it. "Oh, dear."

"It's been several years since my dad was murdered. When I took the law into my own hands, it was the most surreal moment of my life! For the first time I felt really, really powerful. The world was at my fingertips. There was nothing, human or otherwise, that I couldn't buy. Well, so I thought."

"The root of all evil, me boy!"

"It was about five years ago. J.P.S. was celebrating another strong year at our annual Christmas party. David Liebowitz, my SVP of Marketing introduced me to his new hire, Melissa O'Connell."

Elegantly dressed men and women had sat enjoying cocktails while they mingled in a banquet hall at the Beverly Wilshire Hotel. A live band had been playing in the background, creating a perfect atmosphere for the evening party. Hired help made their rounds with hors d'oeuvres.

Martini in hand, Jim swaggered past David's table. He didn't think David noticed him; the boy was engrossed in a conversation with the brunette sitting opposite him at his table. Their table, just like other tables in the banquet hall, was decorated with cocktails and appetizers.

'Oh,' David called out to him. 'Jim, there's someone I'd like you to meet.'

Jim turned toward David's table. He gave the woman a once-over, concluding she was the person he was to meet. He put his charm to use, luring her in with his charismatic presence. Melissa bashfully conversed through body language, revealing more and more skin as she crossed her legs, letting her skimpy dress ride up her thighs. The dress had an exaggerated v-neck, flaunting enough cleavage to ooze sex appeal.

'Jim,' David introduced, 'this is Melissa O'Connell, my new hire.'

Done chewing on his appetizer, he dabbed his mouth with his table napkin. He went on with the introduction, 'Melissa, this is Jim Powers—our President and CEO, my boss.'

Melissa extended her hand, flashing Jim a seductive smile. 'How do you do?'

Her voice was soft, almost musical. Jim took her hand in his and softly kissed it, relishing its tenderness. His gaze darted to her breasts, and he wondered if they were just as soft as the rest of her skin. Perhaps softer?

A wedding ring glittered on her finger, earning his attention. From the corner of his eye, he could see David in a comatose state as he marveled at the sensual beauty sitting beside him.

Jim smiled at her as he released her hand. David hadn't stopped staring. It was no secret he had a thing for her. The look in his eyes had been a little more than professional; it was a look that said he would not resist if she wanted to get him laid.

"Were they having relations?" Father Tim asked in the present.

"At that point," Jim said, "no. Although, they did have an affair during the course of their business relationship."

"Oh," Father Tim mouthed.

"David excused himself and she and I started talking. We sat close, talking, smiling, laughing. She told me her husband was home sick with the flu. My translation of that was 'I want to have sex with you'. I made sure her cocktail glass was never empty. She started opening up to me...I mean *really* opening up to me."

He recalled their playful conversation.

Melissa's laugh flitted across his memory. He remembered she'd grabbed his arm as she laughed with embarrassment, her cheeks flushing.

Her words echoed in his head. *'Oh, my God! I can't believe you'd ask me that!'*

And then his question. *'Well?'*

A giggle, and then a whisper. *'Yeah, just a little. Well, maybe more than a little.'*

● ● ●

"She admitted fantasizing about being with another woman," Jim recalled. "She said she suppressed those feelings based on her Catholic upbringing. And when I asked if she loved her husband, you know what her answer was?"

Father Tim shook his head, blank-faced.

Jim huffed. "It wasn't exactly a yes. She loved him no more than a friend. She only agreed to marry him because he fit the mold. Catholics marry Catholics and bla bla bla. But the love wasn't there. Never had been."

Father Tim's mouth fell open. "That is very disconcerting. I actually performed their wedding ceremony. They seemed very happy."

"A lot of things aren't what they seem, Father," Jim said.

"Apparently, not."

"The party was held at a very prestigious hotel and I, of course, had a penthouse suite available to me. I invited her over, an' she boldly declined. I tried to sway her into goin' with me, and even when I offered her a thousand dollars for just an hour of her time, she stood her ground, telling me she was married. I wasn't used to being rejected and my blood was beginning to boil. What she didn't realize was that within minutes, she'd be in a hotel room with absolutely no recollection of what was about to transpire."

"You drugged her?" Father Tim asked.

"Actually, David did."

"I don't follow?"

"While we were still talking, she passed out at the table. I figured she'd had too much to drink. It happens. So, when David returned and saw her out cold, I eluded all awkwardness as if nothing was wrong. But then he suggested we take her to his room, and at that point I knew exactly what he had done."

Earlier that evening—before David introduced him to her—he'd seen her strut off to the ladies' room, but he'd been too engaged in an important conversation to trail her. Undoubtedly, that was when David had drugged her drink.

Jim sighed resignedly, like he'd had no choice. "I played along."

"So you took her up to his room?" Father Tim probed.

Jim snapped his fingers. "Bingo!"

"And nobody saw this?"

"Shelly Stevens, another one of David's employees saw us carrying her." Jim snickered. "I'm sure others saw, but nobody seemed to be paying much attention to us. It's like they were all in la-la land. Three sheets to the wind, if you catch my drift."

He grew silent, waiting for the question he knew Father Tim would hurl at him. He clasped and unclasped his fingers on the table.

Father Tim spoke after what seemed like an eternity. "I'm afraid to ask—"

"What happened in the room? I've been bottling this up for a long time." His rugged shell began to crack as tears narrowly escaped his stoic eyes. He breathed out his demons as he lowered his head in shame. "We took her up to David's room."

An image of Melissa lying comatose on the bed, limbs dangling off the side, zipped through his head.

"I had him know I was aware he drugged her," Jim continued. "It was a really dangerous drug, unlike any date-rape drug you've heard of. When taken, you pass out. When you wake up, you're still cognizant of your surroundings, but you experience temporary amnesia. You can't remember anything that transpired within twenty-four to forty-eight hours of ingesting the drug. It's almost like those one or two days never even existed. Permanently erased from your memory.

Most people wake up from the deep sleep within about twenty to thirty minutes of passing out. If you take too much of the drug, you're done."

"Did she wake up?" Father Tim asked.

"Yeah, she woke up and saw us both standing there. She had no idea where she was or who we were. I lied about being her husband and David being a doctor. Told her she'd fallen down and hurt herself and the nice doctor was only there to examine her. She bought none of that. And when she screamed, the only way I could shut her up was..." He shrugged one shoulder. "Well, by knocking her out. I had him restrain her, and then I delivered a blow to her stomach."

Memories of Melissa collapsing to her knees invaded his thoughts. Following it was a memory of him smashing her head with a lamp. He shuddered as he remembered the blood trickling from her bruised skull.

"I had him undress her, Father," Jim said. "And just before he excused himself from the room, I had him swear to never say a word about that night. He understood exactly what I meant and never uttered a single word to anyone after that."

"Is the girl still alive?" Father Tim asked.

Jim sighed. "When David left the room, I brutally raped her. There wasn't a single part of her body that I didn't violate. I gagged her so she couldn't scream."

With those words came a forced reliving of what he'd done to her. Gagging her with a necktie, he'd violently raped her, the subtle thrashing of her body and her soft moans intoxicating him. She'd lay unresponsive underneath him, her limbs spread out as he penetrated her in her state of woozy submission.

"She was conscious," he explained, "but woozy. When I was done with her, I inserted the barrel of the gun into her vagina and pulled the trigger."

"Oh, my Lord!" Father Tim said.

• • •

"There was no ammo," Jim said, his words bringing relief to Father Tim. "I just wanted to watch her squirm. The whole entire time, I was thinking of Gus and what I was going to do to him. Every ounce of rage that I felt for him was taken out on this innocent woman. She survived and doesn't remember a thing about it. As far as she and her husband know, she had a real bad accident that night. We even smashed up her car to tie the pieces together. Nobody ever probed and nobody, other than David, knows otherwise. Her memory is fine now, but she'll never remember the forty-eight-hours surrounding the attack. That's how the drug works. Well...at least, that's how it's supposed to work."

"Does she still work at your firm?"

"Well, not anymore. I had David let her go. I started getting vibes that she was having flashbacks of that night...like maybe the drug wasn't fool proof. It's hard to explain...the more she saw me around the office, the colder she became. It's probably my paranoia, but I thought it would be best to get rid of her and not take any chances. If she no longer saw my face, she would no longer have anything to connect it to. There's a certain line that the authorities won't cross when turning a blind eye to evil. That is one of them. That was not something I could pay my way out of."

"And this is something that's been eating you up inside?" Father Tim asked.

Jim shuddered at his bestiality. "I will never stop feeling guilty until the day that I die. Thoughts of suicide are an everyday occurrence. Drugs and alcohol help me forget. I can't give her back what was taken from her. Her husband owes me a lot of money. He's a worthless drug addict. He has no idea that I'm actually the father of her children. He's a real piece of work and I have no respect for him. Melissa deserves better. She trusted me. She trusted David. We both took advantage of her."

He lowered his head and let out a frustrated sigh. He peeked at Father Tim through thick lashes—some of which had turned gray. He'd half-expected Father Tim to be judgemental after hearing the story of how horrible he'd been. But there was none of that in his eyes. The only emotions Jim found there were sympathy and understanding, both coated in an undeserving fatherly love.

"Close your eyes, Jim," Father Tim said. "Let's pray for God's forgiveness."

He reached across the table for Jim's hands. Tentatively, Jim grasped the priest's wrinkled hands and breathed deeply through his mouth. He watched Father Tim close his eyes, and then he followed suit.

"O Lord Jesus Christ," Father Jim started, "mighty God and redeemer—"

Jim's ears twitched at the sound of a bullet shattering the window. His eyes flew open and he leapt to his feet just as the bullet came hissing in his direction.

"Watch out!" he warned.

But the bullet had already pierced through the left side of Father Tim's head, cracking open his skull.

With a prayer on his lips, Father Tim's lifeless torso fell flat on the table. His hands stayed outstretched before him, with his head resting between them. Blood streamed from the side of his head, instantly pooling around him and streaking down the table.

Jim's left leg vibrated as his phone rang. Hands trembling with rage, he located the phone in his pocket and held it to his ear.

"I could easily kill you right now," Gus' voice sailed into his ears, "but how much fun would that be? Your buddies are in my custody now. How foolish of you to leave them alone in the limo! This could all be over if you'd just cooperate. Give me the fucking money! I'm done playing games."

The line went dead.

Jim looked through the shattered glass window, then at his phone. His fingers tightened around the phone, as though he might smash it with his bare hands. The veins on his neck bulged dangerously, complimenting the wooden look in his eyes. His chest tightened and he clenched his teeth. Straight-faced, he returned the phone to his pocket.

CHAPTER ELEVEN

Series of investigations following Stephanie's statement had led Detective Palmer to a possible suspect and his cohorts. Letting in the deceased man's date on his findings would not be out of place.

Closing time was long due and the other officers had all left for home, but some unfinished work on his desk held him back. He ran his left hand along one of the photo frames on his desk; it was a seraphic photo of him, his wife and their eight-year-old daughter.

He sighed heavily. Solving Mitch's murder case had shortened the time he spent with his family. And understandably, his wife was starting to get an attitude about him spending less time with her.

There'd been an important function at their daughter's school, and it'd ended three hours ago. Palmer had been invited, but he'd missed it yet again. The piles of work at the office had been impossible to ditch, not even for a second. He'd been trying to put a call through to his wife, and each time he met a dead end. He could smell a familiar silent treatment from a distance. He sighed, trailing his fingers along his cheekbones with his eyes closed in deep concentration. With a subtle shake of his head, he narrowly opened his eyes and took a swig of the energy drink on his desk.

"Forgive me, Janice," he said.

He scrolled down his contact list and dialed Stephanie's number. He tapped his desk with his other fingers, waiting for Stephanie to pick up.

• • •

"Hello?" her voice rang from the other end.

"Stephanie," he said into his phone, "it's Detective Palmer."

"Oh, hey!"

"Listen, I think we know who's responsible for Mitch's murder. I'm gonna need to ask you a few more questions, though."

"Oh, my God!" she said. "Of course!"

"It's better if we do this in person," he said. "I can either come to your place or you can come back to the station...whichever works for you."

"Ummm, I can come in tomorrow morning. I would come in tonight, but I've been drinking."

"Why don't I just come over to your place?" he suggested, grabbing his pen and notepad. "What's your address?"

"Oh, uh...eight-one-two-five..."

Palmer jotted down the address as she spoke.

"...East Third Street, Apartment Three-B."

He dropped his pen. "Got it! I'm the only one at the station right now, so give me a few to close up and I'll be right over."

"Sure," Stephanie said. "There's a security system downstairs so I'll buzz you in when you arrive."

"Excellent! See you in a bit." He began to end the call, but an afterthought occurred to him. "Oh, and Stephanie..."

"Yeah...?"

A thin breeze—a lot like the breath of a human—tickled the nape of his neck. He bristled in his seat. Gasping, he whirled around and his eyes caught the glint of a large knife. Rough hands grabbed him by the hair, yanked his head back and slashed his throat wide open. Blood squirting from his slit throat, Palmer fell face-down on his desk. His grip on the phone slackened, letting the phone clatter to the ground. He opened his mouth, coughing up blood and accommodating some gurgling sounds.

The knife-wielding man behind him moved around the desk. His hand covered the notepad and he tore out Stephanie's address, after which he shook off Palmer's blood from the paper. He picked up a framed photo of Palmer standing proudly alongside an unmarked police car. He lay the picture frame face down on the desk.

Palmer drowned in his own blood, his vision cutting into a mass of black and nothingness.

***

"Hello? Detective Palmer?" Stephanie held her phone away from her ear and stared at it, her brows darting to meet between her eyes. She could have sworn she'd heard a thump over the phone. "That was weird."

The call timer continued to tick, but Palmer's end of the call was as still as an unperturbed sea. She hung up and placed the phone on the stool beside her couch. A droopy-eyed Rex sedately lay next to her on the couch.

Stephanie grabbed her half-empty glass of wine from the stool, gulped it down and shot Rex another glance. A downcast growl rumbled in his throat.

Stephanie set down the glass and scooted closer to him. "What's the matter?"

No response from Rex.

She tried another approach. "Want some dinner?"

Stephanie had spent all evening reliving her traumatic experience in the alley, and not once had it crossed her mind to refill Rex's plate. Having a pet again would require some getting used to. Stephanie had figured that out already.

• • •

Rex sat up, weakly wagging his tail.

Stephanie thought again, and then something clicked in her head. She held out her right pointer. "I know! You miss daddy, huh?"

Rex whimpered in response. He leapt off the couch and roamed the apartment, sniffing.

"Don't worry, Rex," she said. "We'll find your daddy! Let's get you some dinner."

Stephanie rose to her feet and proceeded to the kitchen. She opened a pantry door and rummaged through some canned goods. "Shit! I could have sworn I still had a can or two."

She walked over to the refrigerator, confident to find a meal for Rex. A knowing smile claimed her face as she peeked inside.

"Aha!"

She retrieved a ready-made rotisserie chicken from the refrigerator, set the container down on the kitchen counter, and undid the lid. She carved up some chicken, placed it in a bowl and advanced to the living room.

Rex was nowhere in sight.

"Rex?" Stephanie called. "Come on, boy...I have some dinner for you."

She wandered into her bedroom and switched on the light, finding him settling on her bed. "There you are!"

Stephanie sauntered to meet him. She'd barely placed the bowl under his muzzle when he sprang up and grabbed a piece of chicken.

"Good boy," she said.

While Rex chomped the treat, Stephanie retrieved the bowl. She watched him swallow the piece of chicken in one heavy gulp.

• • •

"Good boy!" she cheered again. She turned toward the door. "Come on."

His footsteps thumped behind her as she headed back to the living room. He broke into a sprint, beating her to it. His tail wagged with a feverish excitement and he turned around to watch her. She strolled into the kitchen and set the bowl down on the floor. Rex excitedly dug into his meal.

***

Melissa sat at the desk in her home office, munching some potato chips. Her desktop pinged with a new notification, instantly earning her attention. She popped a chip into her mouth, and dusted her palms. She clicked on a minimized chat window from the taskbar.

It was a new message from Satin_Damsel95. *Hey.*

Melissa smiled, relieved to see her online. She'd been logging in and out every now and then just to catch her online and get some updates on the vacancy she looked forward to filling. She hastily typed a reply.

Hey, beautiful! We meet again! Did you get the resumé? Melissa cracked her fingers as she watched the monitor for a new message.

Satin_Damsel95 was currently typing a message. It popped up after a few seconds. *I sure did! I forwarded a copy to my boss. She wants Melissa to come in for an interview this week. Can you pass on the message?*

A wide grin crossed Melissa's face as she typed back. *Oh, my God! That's awesome! I owe you big time! I'll have Melissa call first thing in the morning. What number?*

A new message from Satin_Damsel95 found the screen. *Ya know what? Just have her meet me at the coffee shop right next to our building. We'll have some coffee and then I'll take her up to meet the boss. I'll send directions.*

● ● ●

That sounds great! I can have her meet you at the coffee shop tomorrow morning? Still grinning, Melissa hit the 'enter' key.

Satin_Damsel95's end of the conversation went dead for a few seconds that stretched into two minutes. Melissa glanced at the recent messages she'd sent her. Had she said anything that could blow her cover? Perhaps something untypical of Chris? Or had her hyper-excitement caused Satin_Damsel95 to grow suspicious? None of those seemed likely, so she shrugged off her worry. The lady was probably preoccupied with something else at the moment.

It took a few more moments for Satin_Damsel's response to lazy into view. *Actually, tomorrow won't work. I have an appointment. How about Tuesday?*

Tuesday seemed fine, Melissa thought. Actually, any day was. She had no job to keep her occupied; neither were there any appointments she had to keep. Her fingers punched the keys. *Perfect! What time?*

Satin_Damsel95 responded. *7:00am?*

Great! See you then! Once Melissa's message delivered, she had a sinking feeling that something was amiss. Only when she glanced at the message a second time did she realize her mistake. She'd been too excited about the prospect of a new job, and for a moment she'd let her mask come off. She sighed. That was a close one. She needed to be more careful next time. She would never forgive herself if she lost this rare opportunity that'd been served to her on a platter.

She quickly backpedalled. *Oops! I meant she'll see you then.*

But Satin_Damsel95 had already sent a *'Huh?'*

Thanks again for your help! Melissa ignored Satin_Damsel95's last message. Hopefully, the lady had waved off the slip as an insignificant error.

● ● ●

Satin_Damsel95's next message confirmed her assumption. *No problem!*

Closely following it was another message from her. *Hey, I need to get going now. I'm expecting someone.*

Melissa smiled teasingly as she typed a response. *Your boyfriend?*

Satin_Damsel95 was quick to reply. *No, silly! Long story. I'll have to fill you in later. Bye, for now, handsome!*

Handsome? Melissa chortled. Her fingers hovered over the keyboard as she tried to assemble her thoughts to form a coherent response. Finally deciding, she typed. *You are such a freaking tease! Catch ya later! Think of me when you take off your clothes tonight. I'll be thinking of you!*

Satin_Damsel95 responded. *Goodnight, Rob!*

***

Stephanie stared at the wall clock in her living room. It was running late. Detective Palmer would be here any minute. Her phone rang almost immediately, and she strode over to the desk on which her laptop and stationery resided. She'd left her phone on the desk while sorting through her mail. She picked it up from the desk and answered the call, half-expecting to hear Palmer's voice.

"Hello?" she said.

"Detective Palmer won't be able to make his appointment this evening," a masculine voice said from the receiver. "Just thought I'd pass on the message."

Stephanie frowned, confused. "Who is..." A dial tone interrupted her. "...this?"

She stared at the phone with grave concern and placed it back to her ear. "Hello...?"

All she heard was a silence so deafening her blood ran cold. She hung up, dead-bolted the front door and secured it with a chain.

She clapped her hands, earning Rex's attention. "Come on, Rex! Bed time."

CHAPTER TWELVE

Vehicles slowed to a halt at an intersection, following the command of the traffic lights overhead. Melissa crossed over to the other side of the street, with a designer handbag flung over her shoulder. Chin lifted and shoulders rolled back, her stride was reminiscent of a runway model. Her long brown coat flapped in the wind, revealing a sensual mesh cleavage dress underneath.

A man wolf-whistled from his car as she walked past him. He stuck out his head. "Hey, gorgeous! Can I get your number?"

"Drop dead, asshole!" Melissa said, flashing him her middle finger.

She heard some other people snicker, but she made no attempt to look at them. She pranced into a coffee shop across the road and swept her eyes around, searching for a familiar face—the face she'd seen in the explicit photos. But that face was nowhere to be seen.

From the corner of her eye, a waving arm captured her attention. The arm belonged to an attractive blonde, but not the same blonde she was expecting to meet. The blonde was enjoying a beverage off to the side. She seemed to be in her late twenties. Could this be Satin_Damsel95? Well, there was only one way to find out.

Melissa smiled, approaching the blonde. She halted at her table. "Are you..." An awkward pause followed as she tried to remember a name. "Satin_Damsel95?" She covered her face with embarrassment. "Oh, my God... I don't even know your name!"

The blonde giggled, extending her hand for a shake. "Hi, I'm Stephanie. Great to meet you!"

Melissa grasped the outstretched hand with a charming smile. "Yeah, you too!"

She wasn't terribly surprised to see a face different from the girl in the photos. After all, what professional woman would be reckless enough to email a nude photo of themselves to a complete stranger?

"Have a seat," Stephanie offered, pointing to the seat across from her. "What can I get ya? My treat."

"Oh...I'm okay, actually...thanks!" Melissa flung her coat and handbag over the chair as she sat down. She stared at Stephanie some more. Her screen name indicated she was twenty-three years, but the image of her in reality told a completely different story. She struck Melissa as one in her late twenties, getting ready to climb into her thirties.

"You have a great figure!" Stephanie said.

"Aw," Melissa said, "thank you so much! So do you. How do you know Chr—I mean, Rob?"

Getting used to Chris' made-up name would need some getting used to, Melissa realized.

"Oh! Uh...we're just friends. Online friends." Stephanie leaned in close and lowered her voice. "This is kinda embarrassing, but I make a little extra money chatting online. Nothing nefarious or anything. It's just entertainment." She sipped her coffee. "The cost of living here in L.A. is—"

Melissa cut her off mid-sentence. "Tell me about it! No need to explain. A girl's gotta do what a girl's gotta do."

Stephanie breathed a sigh of relief at the apparent understanding of her questionable side job.

Melissa's thoughts drifted to Chris. If he ever had a chance to meet Stephanie, nothing would get in the way of him getting into her pants. She'd been with him long enough to know his soft spot. And Stephanie was it. He would never be able to get his hands off those soft mounds on her chest. She couldn't blame him, though. The lady was quite a sight. Melissa could bet she was good in bed. Had to be.

"You okay?" Stephanie asked, watching her.

Melissa shook off her thoughts. "Oh! I'm sorry. It's just..." She scrambled for the perfect excuse. "...you look really familiar to me."

Stephanie grinned. "Ya know, I get that all the time! I've been told I look like Jennifer Aniston."

Melissa laughed agreeably. "Yeah, maybe that's it."

"Why don't we head over to the office and I'll introduce you to Charlene?" Stephanie gulped down the last of her coffee.

Melissa's face lit up. "Sure! Hey, thanks again for helping me with this. I really appreciate it."

They both stood up.

"My pleasure, really," Stephanie said. "We need the help."

Melissa followed Stephanie out of the coffee shop, and into the building beside it. Stephanie led her to an office where a bespectacled woman sat at a desk, typing on her keyboard while carrying on a phone conversation. The woman was elegantly dressed in a pencil dress. Although her face was coated in a layer of makeup, Melissa could still see some wrinkles peeking through. That and her thinning voice gave Melissa an idea of the woman's age. Sixties, she concluded.

"You did?" she said into the phone. She went quiet, listening to the person she was on the phone with. She burst into laughter, her eyes crinkling. "Oh, my Lord! You are too cute, my little cupcake. Listen, sweetie...I'm flying out there in a couple of weeks for the holidays, so I'll see you then. Give mommy a great big kiss from me and I'll see you soon."

She listened again, smiling.

"Aw," she said. "I love you too, honey. Bye for now."

She hung up and returned to her typing, oblivious to Stephanie and Melissa in the doorway. Stephanie cleared her throat, announcing their presence.

Startled, the woman looked up at them. "Oh! I'm sorry, I didn't see you two standing there. I was just talking to my grandson. It's his birthday today. Five-years-old, already!"

"Oh, my gosh!" Stephanie said with a labored enthusiasm. "How time flies!"

Eyes rolling, she shook her head as the woman returned half her attention to the monitor.

"Charlene, this is Melissa O'Connell," Stephanie said, "the girl who's applying for the position."

Charlene looked up at Melissa with a formal smile. "Oh, hi Melissa!"

"Good morning," Melissa said.

"Please come in," Charlene said. "Take a seat."

"I'm gonna head over to my desk and get to work," Stephanie said. "Good luck, Melissa."

Melissa watched Stephanie walk away, then turned around to find Charlene reading a printed copy of her resumé. Charlene glanced up at her.

"You obviously have ample experience in the financial sector," Charlene said, removing her eyeglasses, "processing, underwriting, marketing, account executive." She flashed Melissa a serious look. "You ever considered sales?"

"A loan originator?" Melissa asked. "Nah, I don't do well on commission. With two kids, my nerves couldn't handle it."

Charlene giggled. "I totally understand! I raised my little girl with absolutely no help from her father. Full-time job, school. You do what ya gotta do."

"You look really young to have grandkids!" Melissa pointed out.

"Well, thank you!" Charlene said. "I like you already."

CHAPTER THIRTEEN

Chris and David sat back-to-back on the concrete floor of a large warehouse. Naked and gagged, they were chained to one another, with pillars of stacked boxes towering over them on either side. Gus casually sat in a chair, the gleam in his eyes flaunting his enjoyment as he watched them struggle to break free. They'd been at it for hours now, and although their struggles had gotten them nowhere, they pushed ahead.

Gus lit a cigarette and stood up. "That's heavy-duty stainless steel, gentlemen. You ain't never breaking outta there. All I need is a little cooperation. Nod your heads if you're willing."

Chris nodded in a puppet-like fashion. David barely moved a muscle. Eyes narrowed at David, Gus pranced across the room to stand in front of him.

"I guess you enjoy being tied up to a naked man? Fucking faggot! You're a pretty good looking guy, so I'm gonna give you one last chance before I rearrange your face." Gus raised his voice as he continued. "Are you willing to cooperate?"

David nodded reluctantly, his downcast eyes looking anywhere but at Gus. Gus exposed a bloody knife, inched it toward David's face, and cut off his gagging device with it. Flashing a sickening smirk, he pulled out a set of car keys and dangled them in David's face.

"Nice ride," Gus said. "What is it...six-hundred grand?"

David pleaded the fifth, his eyes following the jingling keys.

• • •

"It's on its way to Mexico right now," Gus said, "completely stripped. Not a bad 'keep your mouth shut' gift. Seems to me you are faced with a pretty fucked up dilemma. Your boss, who isn't here to protect you, wants you to keep your mouth shut. I, on the other hand, want you to start talking. Now, I'm no genius, but the way I see it...I have the upper hand here. Would you agree?"

David pondered for a moment, his brows crinkling in concentration. "Doesn't matter. I'm dead either way."

Gus snickered. "Well, let's see. If you don't help me...I'll kill you. If you do help me, your boss will kill you. If you help me and we kill your boss, you live."

***

Buried behind a mountain of files, Stephanie typed at her computer. Animated footsteps perforated the near-silence at the office and she causally raised her head to see an excited Melissa advancing to her cubicle.

"Oh, my God!" Melissa said in a shrill voice. "Oh, my God! Oh, my God! I got the job! I start at the beginning of the month!"

Stephanie leapt to her feet, embracing her in a congratulatory style. "That is so awesome! Okay, we have to celebrate! We need to go out for drinks before you start!"

"That sounds great!" Melissa said, grinning.

Stephanie doubled over and grabbed a business card from her drawer. She handed it over to Melissa. "Here's my card. Call me when you're free, and we'll figure out where to go and when."

Melissa glanced at the business card and placed it in her purse. "Um, sure. I don't have a card to give you, but let me give you my cellphone number."

"Here you go..." Stephanie handed her another card and a pen. "Write it on the back of this."

Melissa grabbed a pen from the desk and jotted down her phone number. "You have no idea how much this means to me! Thank you so much!"

Dropping the pen, she returned the card to Stephanie.

"Hey," Stephanie said, "my pleasure! Okay, I'll get back to this mountain of work. I look forward to seeing you again, preferably behind a Cosmo."

"Ditto! Well, not the mountain of work, but the other. See ya soon." With a broad smile, Melissa strutted off.

***

Chris and David remained chained to one another. Gus casually leaned against a beam, clipping his fingernails. A lit cigarette dangled from his mouth, distorting his face behind a cloud of thick smoke. Wide eyed, Chris watched his every move, conflicting within himself whether to speak or stay silent.

He chose the former. "Hey, pal! I thought you were gonna set us free? We said we'd cooperate.

Gus ignored him.

"Hey!" Chris yelled. "I'm talking to you!"

"Shut the fuck up!" David chided. "You're gonna get us both killed."

Gus dragged on his cigarette, threw it to the ground and calmly approached Chris and David. "Hey, Roaming_Cobra who ain't so roaming! You're awfully demanding for someone in your situation. Maybe you should take your friend's advice and shut the fuck up!"

Chris furrowed his brows. "How do you...?"

Gus cut him off. "I've been watching you and your wife for a long time, you little prick! I know more about the two of you than you know about each other!"

Chris squeezed his eyes shut, letting teardrops stream down each cheek. "I really need to go to the bathroom, man, please! I'm hungry, I'm thirsty, I'm cold. We've been chained up for way too long now. Please, show a little mercy."

Gus looked at his watch, and then he bent down in front of Chris. "Show a little mercy? Maybe you need to show a little respect! A little dignity! You fucking pussy! I'm not so sure I can trust you gentlemen yet. Besides, in case you haven't noticed, we're in a fucking warehouse. This ain't no five star hotel and there sure as hell ain't no bathroom here."

Unzipping his pants, he continued, "When I need to take a piss, I do it right here on the floor."

He sprayed a hot stream of urine on Chris, drenching his unclad body. Chris clenched his eyes and mouth shut so the liquid wouldn't make it to either of those places. Dehumanized, he whimpered as he heard the sound of Gus zipping his pants. His eyes and mouth stayed clamped shut. He feared a sip of urine would sneak into his mouth if he opened it just yet.

"If you need to go that bad, you'll go right now."

Chris pried his eyes open, but played deaf to Gus' words.

"Do it!" Gus barked, causing Chris to flinch.

Chris, a broken man, forced himself to urinate. As much as he found it derogatory to free his bladder this way, he appreciated the soothing relief that followed right after. Behind him, he could feel David straining against the chains. But there was no escaping. Without a choice, they both sat in a puddle of urine.

"I'm gonna be honest with you, Chris," Gus said. "I really don't have a need for you. Now, I'd like to set you free, but I don't trust you. You ever thought about suicide when there's nowhere else to go? Of course you have. You see, sometimes we come to the realization that we're already living in hell. I mean, think about it. Do you really think that hell is any worse than this? Death is very peaceful. You will feel no pain ever again. No responsibilities, no worries, no more crying, nothing!"

He paused, giving Chris a moment to assimilate every word he'd uttered.

"How about it, pal?" he asked.

Gus watched Chris, waiting for a response that never came. He whipped out a gun, aimed it at Chris, then he let out a frustrated sigh.

"Obviously, it wouldn't be suicide if I pulled the trigger and clearly, your hands are tied up at the moment." Doubled over, he carefully positioned the gun upside down between Chris' feet and aligned the barrel between his eyes.

He looked up, locking eyes with Chris. His gaze was laden with meaning. "I'll hold it steady...I think you know what to do."

"Wait!" David yelled, his voice unsteady. "If he ducks, that shit's going straight into the back of my head!"

He struggled against the chains. When his efforts proved futile, he grunted his frustration and leaned his now sweaty body into Chris'.

"He won't duck," Gus said. "Trust me. He's tried it before. Can't even do *that* right."

Chris strategically inched his big toe toward the trigger, his muscles straining in concentration. Once his toe touched the trigger, he squeezed his eyes shut, his heart hammering his chest as he braced himself for the blow. Images ran across his head, the memories overwhelming. His twin boys...he would never see them again. He would die a humiliating death— unclad and in a pool of sweat, blood and urine. An image of his lifeless body struck him and he winced. Melissa's melodic laughter echoed in his ears as flashes of memory of her playing with their kids gripped him.

Sucking in lungfuls of air—the last he would ever breathe—he slowly pressed the trigger.

The gun clicked.

And in that moment, the whole world seemed to freeze.

He waited for the death blow—a blow that would never come.

Gus erupted in laughter, the raucous sound of his voice forcing Chris' eyes open. Chris watched disbelievingly as Gus picked up the gun and straightened his spine. Taking a step back, he opened the chamber of the gun and held it out for Chris to see—it was empty.

Gus broke out of his amusement. He cleared his throat, composing himself. "Ya know, if I had the choice between life in prison or the death penalty, I'd choose death as well. Unfortunately, those bastards on death row sit there for God knows how many years appealing the decision while people like you line up every day to take their own lives. Pretty twisted, really. They want to live and you want to die. I guess going against one's wishes really is the worst punishment. I think we'll keep you around for a bit."

He stepped back again.

"Jesse!" he yelled, facing the door. "Rubin! Bring these guys some food and water." He turned toward Chris and David. "Don't worry fellas, we'll escort you to a restroom if need be. Don't need this place smelling like a toilet."

He slithered off toward the exit. "I'll be back.

CHAPTER FOURTEEN

Dressed in a tight-fitting leather skirt and an off-shoulder top, Stephanie paraded down the streets of Beverly Hills. The evening breeze whispered in her ears. Her hand vibrated and she looked down at her purse, retrieving her ringing cellphone from it.

"Hello," she said into her phone.

"Hey it's Melissa," a voice from the phone said.

"Oh, hey!" Stephanie said.

"How's it going with work?" Melissa asked. "You done?"

"Yeah, I'm done." Stephanie glanced down at her watch. It was 6:10 p.m. Her eyes locked on a local restaurant/bar across the street as she raised her head. On the face of the building, an illuminated signboard shed a warm aquamarine light on the street. On the signboard, the name 'Mastro's Steakhouse' was boldly written in a majestic font.

"Do you know where Mastro's is?" Stephanie asked.

"Uhm..." Melissa pondered for a moment. "Yeah, I sure do."

"Great! See you in a bit." Stephanie hung up. She innocently jaywalked across the street, left hand held in the air, oblivious to an oncoming car speeding in her direction. The car screeched to a halt and honked at her. Successive horns blared all around the street.

The driver in the halted car poked his head out of the window. "Hey, lady. What the hell are you doing?"

• • •

"Sorry," Stephanie said sheepishly.

She vacated the main road and strutted off into the bar area of Mastro's. Scoping out the joint as she walked in, she walked over to an empty booth in the corner and plopped down on one of the chairs. She leaned back into the chair, watching Liz, an attractive cocktail waitress make her rounds.

"I'll be over in just a moment to take your order," Liz said.

"Take your time, Liz," Stephanie said. "I'm in no hurry."

Liz smiled at Stephanie, and then she turned away to place a customer's order. Stephanie busied herself by checking her email on her phone and replying to new messages. It took a few minutes for Melissa to show up.

"Hey." Melissa slid into the chair across from her.

"Hi," Stephanie said. She stuck a lock of hair behind her right ear.

"I take it you come here often?" Melissa asked, shifting into a more comfortable position. Finding one, she crossed her legs at the knees.

Stephanie nodded with slight reservation. "Yeah. I was supposed to have dinner here the other night, and well—"

"Wait...that was you?" Melissa's startled voice cut her off. "Oh, my God! I saw that on the news. I thought you looked familiar."

Stephanie lowered her head and squeezed her eyes shut as tears sought to break her. Memories of Mitch's murder flooded her, wrenching her heart. But warmth seeped into her as Melissa reached across the table and clenched onto her hand.

"Everything will be okay, sweetie," Melissa said, her voice soft and comforting. "I promise."

Stephanie raised her head. She squeezed Melissa's hand back and breathed deeply, willing her hurt away, at least for a moment. Melissa cracked her a weak smile.

* * *

"Thanks, hon'," Stephanie said. "It was almost fate that we met, although not surrounding the greatest circumstances."

"Everything happens for a—" Melissa started, but Liz' presence cut her off. She slipped her hand away from Stephanie's and straightened her spine.

Liz grinned at Stephanie. "Hey, Steph! It's really good to see you. I heard about what happened. How are you doing?"

"Eh!" Stephanie said. "I'm as well as I can be. Hangin' in there, trying to stay positive."

She smiled stiffly.

"And so you should!" Liz said. She looked between the two women. "What can I get you ladies?"

Melissa picked up a cocktail menu lying on the table and glanced through it.

Stephanie began to place her regular order, but then she clicked her tongue, deciding against it. "Ya know what? I'm going to try something different tonight! We're celebrating Melissa's new job!"

Melissa smiled bashfully at Liz.

Liz returned a broader smile. "Congratulations!"

"Thank you." Melissa returned her attention to the cocktail menu.

"Give me an A.M.F," Stephanie said, stifling a laugh.

A stern look crossed Liz's face as though she were just about to scold a brat. She stood akimbo. "Steph, what do you *really* want?"

Melissa blinked. "What's an A.M.F.?"

Stephanie exchanged a mischievous look with Liz, then leaned in close to Melissa.

"It stands for 'adios, motherfucker!'" she said quietly.

Melissa erupted into laughter. "Oh, that's rich! Tell ya what. If you finish it, I'll buy you another one!"

"Deal!" Stephanie laughed too.

Melissa schemingly looked up at Liz. "I'll have a glass of Chardonnay, please."

"Comin' right up!" Liz said.

"Can you excuse me for a moment?" Stephanie asked.

Melissa dropped the menu. "Sure."

Stephanie rose from the chair, adjusted her skirt and headed into the ladies room. Her reflection in the mirror caught her eye, and she stood in front of it, briefly admiring herself. She was utterly exhausted from work, yet her baby blue eyes were as piercing as ever. She proceeded into a stall and locked the door. Hitching up her skirt so it gathered around her waist, she sat on the toilet seat and breathed a sigh of relief as she did her business. She tugged off a few sheets of toilet paper.

She paused at the sound of a creaking door, her ears twitching with alertness. A moment of silence closely followed the creak. Slow, heavy methodical footsteps proceeded the silence. The footsteps disappeared into an adjacent stall, and a pin-drop silence blanketed the ladies room as the door slammed shut. Stephanie furrowed her brows at how ridiculous she'd been. This was a public place, and it wasn't out of place for people to stroll in and out just like she'd done. She wiped herself clean, vacated the toilet seat and flushed the waste down the drain.

Stephanie exited the stall, and although she trusted nothing could go wrong, she tossed a cautious glance around the room. There was no one in sight. This should give her some measure of calmness, but it didn't—not when all but one stall was wide open.

She crept to the sink, her reasoning shrouded in unease. She washed her hands, wiped them clean and tossed the used paper towel into a trashcan. Done, she turned to leave. A piercing scream threw her lips apart as she stood nose-to-nose with Gus.

Gus was quick to stifle her scream with a hand to her mouth. "I thought I told you not to go to the cops."

She grabbed his arm and yanked it away from her mouth. Her eyes burned with bitter resentment. "What the fuck are you doing? You scared the shit out of me! Jesus Christ!"

"What's the matter?" he teased. "You don't like surprises?"

"Not in the ladies room!" she hissed.

"So, were you able to get what we need from her?" he asked.

"Not yet," she said. "But I'm getting close."

"You're so sexy when you're angry. Gimme a kiss." He leaned in for a kiss.

She sidestepped, dodging him. Her face puffed up with amusement. "Gus, someone is going to see you in here. Later!"

"Okay, baby," he said. "Just remember to follow the plan. We can't afford to screw this up."

"I know, I know. Let me get back to my—" She signaled quotation marks, "—'friend'. I'll catch ya later."

Without waiting for his response, she headed toward the door.

"Hey Steph!" Gus called after her.

Halting, she turned around to face him.

"About Mitch," he said. "I'm sorry you had to witness that. I have to admit, though...that was some pretty good acting. You were quite convincing in front of Jesse and Rubin." He chuckled. "You looked really scared."

Stephanie received the compliment with a weak smile. "Well, it had only been a few days since you and I met. I wasn't sure that I could trust you. I *was* scared."

"Did he, uh...look familiar to you at all?" Gus asked.

"Ummm...no." Stephanie thought for a moment, and then she shrugged. "I mean...maybe. Why?"

She quirked a brow at him, waiting for him to snuff out her piqued curiosity. She thought back to her first reaction when she met Mitch for the first time. He'd looked somewhat familiar, and he'd made the same comment about her as well. Sure, she looked familiar to everyone who'd seen Jennifer Aniston. And Mitch—well, she still couldn't figure out why he'd looked familiar. But what did that have to do with anything? And what did it matter to Gus?

"No reason." Gus dismissively replied. "Let's get outta here."

She exited with a hint of guilt on her face. But she shook it off like a piece of unwanted clothing, as though she hadn't walked her date to a gruesome death. It would be a while before she forgot him, though. The only thing he'd been to her was nice.

CHAPTER FIFTEEN

The bar had come alive within the past hour. Jam-packed and loud, it now buzzed to life as an upbeat jazz band played in the background. The band consisted of four suited men with matching black hats, and a female vocalist who was elegantly dressed in a floor-sweeping slit red dress. Melissa sat across from an inebriated Stephanie. She watched the band as they performed. The guitarist leaned backward as he strummed his instrument, adding rhythm to the song. Behind him, the pianist slammed his fingers into the black and white keys on the piano keyboard, his head slowly rocking to the rich resonating music he produced.

Liz walked over to Melissa's table, the blaring music all but muffling her footsteps. "Can I get you girls anything else?"

Melissa had had enough drinks for one night. She looked over to Stephanie in her giddy state. It was apparent she'd reached her drinking threshold. One more glass and she'd snap.

"She's already had four of those blue drinks," Melissa said pointedly. "And three glasses of chardonnay are more than enough for me. Just the check, please."

"What do you mean?" Stephanie asked, her voice slurring toward incoherence. "I'm still waiting for my order of lettuce wraps and my drink. We're not going anywhere!"

"Honey, we're leaving and you're not drivin'." Melissa outstretched her hand toward Stephanie. "Hand me your purse."

"No!" Stephanie leaned away, casting her a weary look.

• • •

"I'm trying to help you," Melissa said in a hushed voice. She leaned across the table toward Stephanie. "Hand me your fucking purse or I will take it from you. Your choice."

Stephanie laughed impishly.

"You're cute when you get mad." With a robotic move, she threw her purse at Melissa who caught it with a jerk. "Take my stupid purse. See if I care."

Melissa rummaged through the purse and pulled out a wallet.

"Are you stealing my money?" Stephanie asked, her voice becoming even slurrier.

Melissa chortled. She found Stephanie's driver's license and held it up for her to see. "No, I'm looking for this."

She shifted in her seat so she faced Liz. "Hi, I'm so sorry to bother you, but I really need to get Stephanie home. Here's her address." She presented the driver's license to Liz, letting her eyes roam its contents. "Any chance you can give me some directions? I don't know the neighborhood all that well."

Recognition sparkled in Liz's eyes. "Absolutely! I know exactly where this is. Do you have a pen?"

"One moment," Melissa said. She remembered seeing something like a pen in Stephanie's purse. She rummaged through it again and her fingers locked around a pen. "Got it!"

She handed the pen to Liz who jotted down directions on a napkin.

Done writing, Liz handed over the pen and napkin with a sympathetic smile. "Shouldn't take you more than fifteen minutes or so to get there."

"Thank you so much!" Melissa said. She glanced at the napkin. The directions seemed clear enough. "I guess those drinks really do live up to their name, huh?"

● ● ●

Stephanie expelled a projectile vomit, splattering the unclean liquid all over the table. She cried in humiliation, her hands scrambling for a napkin to wipe her mouth with.

"It's okay, hon'," Melissa said. "Let's get you home."

"I'll clean it up," Liz offered. "Not the first time this has happened."

***

Liz had been right. Arriving at Stephanie's apartment had taken no more than fifteen minutes, and her clear directions had made it easy for Melissa to locate it. Now she lay on a couch in Stephanie's living room, with the moonlight dimly illuminating the room in the absence of artificial lights.

Melissa was down to her undergarments, with a throw pillow wedged between her legs in a futile attempt to soothe a steadily building ache down there. She tossed and turned on the couch, her move almost snakelike. She fluffed out a pillow and shook out a blanket. Her cellphone lay beside her on the couch. She flipped it open, eager to know for how long she'd been unable to sleep. The time read: 3:15 a.m.

With a sigh, she rose to her feet. She ambled around the apartment, not exactly searching for anything. But checking on Stephanie didn't seem like a bad idea. She narrowly opened the bedroom door and peered in. The bedroom was just as dimly lit as the living room. She'd turned off the lights herself just after tucking Stephanie into bed. She'd stripped off Stephanie's top, leaving only a bra. Her top had been soiled with vomit and had to go. She'd left the skirt on though—none of the slime had touched it.

Rex was passed out beside Stephanie on the bed. Melissa quietly closed the bedroom door. It clicked shut. She held her breath, slowly turning to catch a reaction from the slumbering pair.

There was none.

She tiptoed into the bathroom and turned on the light, nervously glancing over her shoulder. She flipped open a hamper's lid and rifled through Stephanie's soiled clothes. She spotted Stephanie's thong panties peeking between some dresses. She reached for it and yanked it out. She held the flimsy cotton to her face, breathing in the intoxicating feminine aroma. The ache between her legs had subsided. But now, it returned full force, craving a sensual touch.

As she continued to indulge in her sinful pleasure, she slipped her hand into her panties, drawing slow patterns around her throbbing clit. Her legs parted slightly to accommodate two fingers as she shoved them between her moistness. She gasped, her breath hitching. Her stomach clenched with every shove, spurring her on to keep pumping her fingers inside of her. The murky smell of her arousal toyed with her senses and she slipped out her fingers—they glistened with her natural lubricant. She trailed her lips with her fingers, coating them with her juice. Her lips parted slowly, and she glided her fingers into her mouth to taste herself. She breathed deeply, savoring the taste. Her fingers found the crux of her legs again, kneading and teasing. Now lubricated enough for more, she thrust in three fingers, pumping them in and out with hard thrusts.

Her clit pulsated, craving the feel of a tongue dragging rough taste buds along her rawness.

"Can I help you with something?" Stephanie's voice filtered in from the threshold.

Melissa gasped, her fingers stuck in the swollen folds between her legs. She still had Stephanie's pantie pressed to her nose. She stood with her back to Stephanie, so she hadn't been caught with the underwear. Yet.

With this knowledge as an advantage, she clenched her fist around the pantie and turned around to face Stephanie,

● ● ●

simultaneously dropping the pantie in the hamper. Stephanie stood at the entrance, hands crossed at her chest, with a blank expression on her face.

"Oh my God!" Melissa muttered, her cheeks heating up. "This is embarrassing. I thought you were asleep?"

"Yeah," Stephanie said. "Well...I sobered up. Care to explain yourself?"

"Well—" she started. Her breath caught in her throat and she shrieked, her gaze shooting behind Stephanie. Her face suddenly lost its colors and her eyes were round with fear. "Oh my God! Quick, behind you! There's somebody there!"

Stephanie whirled around, and simultaneously, Melissa grabbed a glass potpourri bowl. She smashed it over Stephanie's head. The bowl exploded into a million shards of glass; they scattered across the floor. Stephanie whimpered, crashing to the floor. She recoiled—apparently pierced by the shards underneath her—and began to scramble to her feet.

"You fucking little cunt!" Melissa raged. "You are going to pay dearly for what you've done. Chris is my husband, you fucking bitch...not my brother! Yeah, Chris. You know his real name. A little extra money on the side? Bullshit! You can drop the charade now. I'm not stupid!"

She grabbed Stephanie by the hair and dragged her along the floor to the bedroom. Glass fragments lodged into Stephanie's skin. She thrashed around, whimpering and struggling to break free. But she stood no chance against a vengeful Melissa. She was just about to find out.

Melissa banged the light switch in the bedroom, and light spilled out of the overhead bulbs. With a startled howl, Rex leapt off the bed.

Melissa snapped her fingers at him, gesturing to the door. "Outta here...go!"

Rex blurred toward the door. He hopped on his hindlimbs, his forelimbs pawing at the doorknob. The door gave way and he bolted out. Melissa marched to the door and slammed it shut. She peeked into Stephanie's closet and yanked out a long black scarf. That should be just enough to restrain her with. Scarf in hand, she returned to Stephanie who was clinging onto consciousness.

"Please," Stephanie cried. "I didn't know."

Slowly heaving her torso off the floor, she pressed her palms into the floor and crept backwards, eager to get away from Melissa. She reached a dead end as her back bumped into the bed. She shrieked, her chest heaving as she sucked in frantic breaths.

Melissa swept Stephanie's listless body off the floor and flung her onto the bed. Stephanie struggled against her as she hastened to unzip her skirt. Overpowering the struggle, Melissa undid the zipper and dragged the skirt down her legs. She ripped off Stephanie's underwear, leaving her completely naked and vulnerable. The flowery sheets underneath Stephanie's head were smeared with blood oozing out of her broken head. She whimpered, trying to fight off Melissa as she straddled her.

Melissa lowered her head, gently gliding her tongue around Stephanie's lips. Stephanie pressed her lips together in disgust.

"I know what your dad did to me that night at the Christmas party," Melissa whispered harshly into Stephanie's ears.

She raised Stephanie's hands above her head and bound them with the scarf. She straightened her spine, her hands creeping to cup Stephanie's breasts. She squeezed them tightly, pinching the pink nipples to inflict pain. Stephanie yelped, her back arching.

"I've been waiting a long time for this opportunity," Melissa said. "I've been quiet and patient. The twenty-five million dollars that you and Gus are trying to extort from your

• • •

dad...it's mine. He owes it to me, Goddamn it! Do you have any idea how it feels to have a gun shoved inside of you?"

She shook Stephanie violently, demanding an answer.

"Do you?"

Stephanie jerked her head to the right. She stayed silent.

Melissa clenched her right fist and held it to Stephanie's face. Stephanie cast it a blank stare.

"You see this?" Melissa asked.

Stephanie's eyes bulged as realization washed over her. She kicked frantically. Melissa smirked; that was exactly the reaction she'd been hoping for.

"No!" Stephanie cried. "No, please!"

Melissa pulled back her arm and flung Stephanie's skinny legs apart. She thrust two fingers into Stephanie. She added a third, wiggling them around until they were fully in. Stephanie moaned and whimpered underneath her. A fourth finger forced its way in. Stephanie tried to clamp her legs shut, but Melissa nudged them, keeping them open. It was a tight fit, but some vigorous wriggling and twisting slowly opened Stephanie up to accommodate all four fingers.

She inched in her thumb, and once all five breached Stephanie's tight ring of delicate flesh, she clenched her hand into a fist and jabbed it up toward Stephanie's stomach. A scream of pure agony tore through Stephanie's shuddering body. Her back arched, sending the top of her head digging into the bed. The dryness between her legs impeded Melissa's progress.

Melissa hissed. Had the circumstances been different she'd scramble for some lubes so her clenched fist would glide in smoothly. But the only emotion she wanted to inflict to the girl underneath her was pain—the same pain that had been meted out on her by Stephanie's father. The veins on Stephanie's neck throbbed as Melissa's fist pumped her hard and rough, stretching her out completely.

CHAPTER SIXTEEN

S pending the night chained to a naked man was far from how David had pictured the end of his day. For hours, he'd helplessly sat in a pool of urine until it totally dried up. But the stench lingered. It was in fact the only smell his assaulted nostrils could pick up. His skin was clammy, glistening with sweat. He could bet on it that the stale sweat coating his back was more of Chris' than his.

Chris had just woken up. He'd managed to get some shuteye during the night. David on the other hand, hadn't been so lucky. His humiliating reality caused sleep to elude him. He bowed his head in shame. His body was starting to stiffen from his immobility, and his hands hurt from being restrained for hours. The cold metal of the steel chains were eating into his skin, scarring him.

A steamy cup of coffee in one hand, and a cigarette in the other, Gus leaned against a support beam in the background. Jesse and Rubin sat at a folding table, engrossed in a game of blackjack.

Gus threw his cigarette to the ground and approached the restrained men. "I'm gonna be real blunt with you fellas. I'm on a time limit to get something done and your cooperation is not only needed; it's mandatory."

David slowly raised his head to look at him. From the movement behind him, he could tell Chris was doing the same.

"David, you are about to make a very important phone call," Gus went on. "If you cooperate and everything goes according to plan, you will be set free and handsomely rewarded..." He sipped his coffee. "...to the tune of five-million dollars."

David stirred at the mention of a reward. He peered into Gus' eyes, trying to deduce if he was telling the truth. It would be a grave mistake to trust this man. He barely even knew him, and so far he'd been anything but trustworthy. Then again, he didn't have much of a choice. He stared warily at him.

"Something you may or may not know about your boss," Gus said. "He has an estranged daughter...Stephanie. They had a huge falling-out several years ago."

"I'm aware," David said.

"You are going to call him and let him know that his daughter is in grave danger in the hands of some really seedy individuals," Gus instructed, "one of which is an ex-employee with a score to settle."

He cocked his head to the side, an evil smirk casting a dark shadow across his face.

"That's right," he continued. "You know who I'm talking about. You will tell him that his daughter is physically unable to call him for help or she'd have done so by now. You will also tell him that he will need to show up at this address..." He set down a handwritten address in front of David. "...at twelve p.m. sharp, with twenty-five million dollars in cash, or he will never see his daughter alive again. Now, I don't really give a shit how you convey this message, but it better be convincing and if you try anything clever..."

Gus aimed his gun at David, his hand on the trigger. Although David knew Gus wouldn't pull the trigger just yet, his heart skipped a beat anyway.

"...you will die," Gus said. "Let him know that when he knocks on the door, a gentleman will open it and he is to hand over the cash...in a briefcase...to him. He must then proceed back to his car and wait for Stephanie to safely be returned into his custody. She will be released exactly five-minutes after the exchange. Do I make myself clear?"

David nodded. He stared at a cellphone—*his* cellphone—as Gus held it inches away from his face.

"Look familiar?" Gus asked, no doubt noting the recognition in David's eyes.

David nodded reluctantly. He watched Gus power up the phone and scroll through the contact list.

"Oh..." Gus said, "I almost forgot the most important part. Tell him Jesse and Rubin turned on me. Snuffed me out with a plastic bag. You can even text him this handy dandy picture in case he questions it." Gus showed David the photo on his phone. It was that of a deceased man bound to a chair with a clear plastic bag secured tightly around his face. There was no mistaking the man in the photo was Gus, feigning his own death in convincing fashion. "I'm dead and have nothing to do with this." He faked a smile. "Okay, you're up."

Gus pressed a button on the cellphone and held it to David's ear.

"Where in the fuck are you?" Jim barked from the phone's loud speaker. "I turn my back for one Goddamn minute, and you—

"Jim," David interrupted, "please. I have something really important to tell you."

Jim's proceeding silence told David he had mellowed down and was ready to listen to him.

"It's about Stephanie," David said. "And...well...here's the deal. She's been abducted and is in grave danger. She'd call you for help, but is unable to. They're gonna kill her if you don't show up at 12 p.m. with twenty-five million dollars."

"That bastard Gus is behind this, isn't he?" Jim probed.

• • •

David swallowed a lump in his throat and looked up at Gus. Gus never lost focus of him. The whole warehouse was dead-quiet, and although Chris, Jesse and Rubin looked anywhere but at David, it was obvious they were craning their ears to hear the outcome.

"Gus has nothing to do with this," David said. "Gus is dead. His two goons turned on him. Suffocated him with a plastic bag."

Gus choked on an overwhelming laughter.

"No no no," Jim said, disbelieving. "This entire conversation reeks of deception. Who else would put you up to making this ridiculous phone call?"

David scrolled through his phone and pushed 'send.' "Look at the picture I just sent you."

The seconds ticked by as David awaited a reaction. His heart pounded through his chest while his eyes darted around the room. How could he betray the man who trusted him most? Nothing seemed to matter anymore. The rules of the game had changed.

Jim expelled a wary sigh, then responded. "I don't know, David. Something isn't adding up here."

Unsure how to respond, David looked to Gus who threw him a 'just-handle-it' look. "Jim...I know you had a falling-out with Stephanie. I also know you love her unconditionally and miss her very much. It doesn't matter why I'm making this phone call. What matters is that if you don't follow these instructions, they are going to kill her. You've already buried your dad...do you really want to bury your daughter as well?"

Silence crept in from Jim's end.

"You are to hand over the cash to the gentleman who opens the door for you," David continued. "They want the bills stacked in a briefcase. And then you're expected to return to your car and wait for Stephanie to be released within the next five minutes."

Again, all he heard from Jim was silence.

"Jim?" he called.

"What address?"

David read the handwritten address.

"Tell them I will be there at noon..." Jim said. "...with the cash."

Gus pulled the phone away from David's ear just as Jim hung up. Surprised by the outcome, David looked up at Gus.

"It's on," David said.

"You will get paid when I get the briefcase." Gus strode out of the warehouse.

David kept staring in Gus' direction even after he was out of sight. Chris' fidgeting behind his back stole his attention. If he didn't know better, he'd think Chris had gotten a key to free himself with. Had he?

It took him only a moment to find out. The padlock binding Chris to him clinked open.

"What about me?" David whispered.

"Sorry, pal," Chris whispered. "I only have one key. The key that opens *your* padlock is with Rubin."

David turned to look at Rubin who flipped him off and vacated the table where he'd been playing blackjack with Jesse. Jesse was nowhere in sight. He'd probably left while David was engrossed in his conversation with Jim. Without sparing him a glance, Rubin made his exit.

Chris quietly stood up. He grabbed the handwritten address on the floor in front of David. "Thanks for setting everything up. You're a real pal."

***

Chris stealthily headed for the exterior of the warehouse. For the first time in hours, he felt the whoosh of fresh air fluttering against his bare skin. Once he made it outside, his stealthy strides broke into a near-sprint as he headed for a '77 Chevy Caprice. Jesse and Rubin stood beside the vehicle, with the trunk wide open.

Jesse yanked out a pile of clothes from the trunk and tossed it to Chris who caught it in one fluid motion. Chris hastily dressed himself—the pile consisted of a gray long-sleeved polo shirt and faded jeans. He hurried to the driver's seat, and Jesse and Rubin simultaneously hopped onto the back seat. Chris turned the ignition just as an enraged Gus barged out of the warehouse.

"Fuck!" Chris yelled, sighting him from the rearview mirror.

The car lurched away from the premises, and Gus relentlessly fired a round of ammo into the car, denting the rear windshield with bullets. Jesse and Rubin ducked instinctively. Breathing hard as he maneuvered the wheel, Chris swerved the car around a corner. The tires screeched as they sped down the road. With Gus now far behind and out of view, Jesse and Rubin straightened their spines.

"That was close," Chris muttered, casting them a glance to see if they were alright. They were unscathed; at least for now.

CHAPTER SEVENTEEN

Gagged with a bandana and bound to a chair in her bedroom, Stephanie still felt raw between her legs. Besides the rawness was a burning sensation inflicted by Melissa's merciless thrusts. Now left with a gaping hole, she was unsure how to position her legs around it. Her legs were parted, and she had a feeling that clamping them shut would soothe the ache. But the ropes binding her legs to the chair didn't give her a chance to. Similar ropes were fastened around her wrists, binding her to the chair so she couldn't move a muscle.

She twisted in the seat, desperately wanting to run a finger through her rawness and massage the pain away. A whoosh of fresh air stole its way in. It should soothe her, but instead it burned, reeking of humiliation. The air blanketed her, causing goosebumps to crawl all over her skin. She shivered. If only she could curl up under the covers, shielding herself from the cold. The curtains billowed as a more ferocious blast of air burst in through the windows. Stephanie gritted her teeth and lowered her head, helpless and defeated.

She raised her head as Melissa ripped a sheet off the bed. She recoiled at the sight of her blood from her head smeared across the top of the sheet. Barely glancing at her, Melissa wrapped the sheet around her body and stepped away, dialing a number on her cellphone. Stephanie whimpered quietly as the sheet teased her bare chest, bringing alive the sting in her nipples she'd tried so hard to ignore. Melissa had bitten her nipples so hard, drawing blood, after which she had sucked on them, numbing the pain.

Despite herself, Melissa's assault had reached a point where it actually felt good to Stephanie. Spread out on the bed, her body had moved on its own, arching toward Melissa's rhythmic thrusts as she dominated her. Shame overwhelmed her as she kept thinking about the scene in bed with Melissa. She'd been raped by a vengeful woman and was not supposed to find it pleasing. But for some reason the pain had been a welcome emotion. Hell, she found it just as ecstatic as being with a man. Probably even more.

Melissa stood by the window, peering out through the blinds. "Shelly, it's me, Melissa. I'm at the apartment. Look, you have got to be one-hundred percent sure that you know what is going to happen today. Twenty-five million dollars split two ways is a shitload of money. Promise me you know exactly what they are going to do?"

A beat of silence passed by as she listened to Shelly's response.

Stephanie lowered her head again.

***

The homeless man stood in front of a building amongst identical structures in an apartment complex. The building was tagged '8125'. He held out a piece of paper and compared the inscription to the building number. It was a match.

He subtly looked to the left, and then to the right, making sure the coast was clear. Vehicles and pedestrians trailed down both sides of the road as typical of middays. Finding nothing questionable, he headed up a flight of stairs toward the main entrance. He tugged on the door and found it locked. He sighed, dialing the manager's office on the residential directory.

"Manager's office," a female voice—apparently the manager's—said from the receiver.

"Uh..." The homeless man paused. He hadn't even thought of a believable lie. Spontaneous words spun around his tongue. "I'm here to do some electrical work."

"One moment," the manager said.

For the next few moments, muffled sounds came from her end of the call. The homeless man concluded she'd cupped her hand over her receiver while confirming his supposed appointment. He tapped his right foot on the floor, giving in to impatience as it slowly seeped into him.

"I'm sorry, sir," the manager's voice found his ear again. "We don't show any electrical work on our log and the building has been evacuated today."

**

"Steph?" Gus called, quietly approaching Stephanie's front door.

He listened for an answer but heard none. He yanked out a bunch of keys from his pocket and unlocked the door with one of the keys. He pushed open the door, eyes scanning the living room as he moseyed in.

His sixth sense kicked in, and he flipped out his gun. He surveyed the living room, his hand on the trigger, ready to fire if he noticed anything out of the ordinary. So far, everything seemed normal.

"Steph, you here?" He took a squint at his wristwatch. Midday was almost upon him.

At the sound of a loud bang on the sliding glass door, he spun toward the balcony, whipping his gun in that direction. He had no idea who he'd expected to find, but it certainly wasn't Rex. Locked outside, Rex barked frantically. Propped up on his hindlimbs, he leaned against the door, with his forelimbs pounding the door as he barked on.

Gus approached Rex, the frown on his face holding a threat. He pounded the glass door with his fist. "Shut the fuck up!"

He drew the curtains, shutting out Rex's image. He advanced to Stephanie's bedroom and turned the doorknob. With a creak, the door opened. Crowding the entrance to the room, Gus heard a feminine moan that could only be Stephanie's.

He found her tied to a chair, struggling to free herself. A bandana was tied between her lips, gagging her. On her body was a bedsheet that had apparently been wrapped around her at some point. Now it lay in a messy bundle on her thighs, baring her totally unclad torso. Her bare legs peeking through from underneath the bedsheet told Gus the rest of her body was just as unclad. Under a different circumstance, he would stand in admiration of her sensual beauty and entertain thoughts of having her in his bed. But now, those thoughts eluded him. Her being tied up could only mean one thing—trouble; more trouble than he'd seen coming.

He exited his train of thought. "What the f—"

A knock at the door caused him to gulp down the rest of his words. He secured his gun into his waistline.

"I'll be back," he said to Stephanie.

Stephanie responded with a strained nod.

Gus strode to the front door and peered through the peephole. Finding Officer Hansen, he opened the door, admitting him inside the house. Hansen was smartly dressed in a formal black suit, giving him an appearance of someone who should be seated behind a desk in a spacious office.

Rex hadn't stopped barking, but with the shut curtains keeping him out of sight, Gus found it less intolerable.

"What the fuck took you so long?" he said to Hansen in a high-pitched voice.

"Hey," Hansen said, holding out both hands, "I'm doing you a favor here. Enough with the attitude, pal."

"Shit!" Gus said, frazzled. "Something isn't right here. The entire fucking plan is unraveling." He touched his temple, willing his disquietude to mellow out. "Okay, we can still pull this off. He is going to be here in about fifteen minutes with the briefcase. When he knocks on the door, you know what to do. If anybody else knocks on the door...and you better use the Goddamn peephole...do not let them in. Follow the plan, and nobody gets hurt. You'll get your money when I get the briefcase. I'll be hiding out in the bedroom."

He stormed off to the bedroom, and without slowing his stride, slammed the door behind him. He headed straight to Stephanie and ripped the bandana from her face. She cried hysterically, breathing in raspy rattles. Her nude breasts clapped against her chest with every sharp breath she sucked in.

"Shut up!" Gus whispered, gluing his fingers to her lips. "Where is she?"

He pulled away his fingers, giving her the go-ahead to speak.

Stephanie hiccupped as she sobbed. "I don't know. She attacked me and raped me...I don't know where she went."

"Oh, that's great!" Gus said, disbelieving. "She attacked you and raped you? You have got to be kidding me! She was supposed to be your pawn, not the other way around. Let me guess...you drank too much?"

"I'm sorry," Stephanie said.

Gus returned the bandana to its place between Stephanie's lips, shutting her up. She gasped as he tied it tightly—perhaps tighter than Melissa had—behind her head.

Stephanie looked up at him, her eyes demanding an explanation. Apparently she'd thought he'd free her right away.

"It's okay, baby," he said, giving her shoulder a gentle pat. "You tried. Just shut your pie hole and let me handle it from here. This will all be over soon and we'll be rich!"

He pulled up the bedsheet and wrapped it around her body, concealing her nakedness. With that, he stormed off.

CHAPTER EIGHTEEN

Chris pulled up the '77 Chevy Caprice in front of Stephanie's apartment building and slammed on the brakes. He turned toward Jesse and Rubin. "If I'm understanding this correctly, there is a guy guarding the front door?"

Jesse and Rubin nodded in agreement.

"Jesse, you go in through the bathroom window and take out the guard," Chris instructed. "Use a knife. Make sure you leave the bathroom window open for Rubin. The apartment is on the first floor, so you shouldn't have a problem getting in. If you happen to run into Gus, take him out immediately! According to the plan, he'll be hiding out in Stephanie's bedroom until the end, so I don't foresee an issue with him. When Jim knocks on the door, open it. Make sure you have your mask on at that point. Take the briefcase and close the door behind him. Have a weapon handy in case he pulls one on you. When Jim gets back into his car, I will call you. Have your phone on 'vibrate.' As soon as you receive the call, get the fuck outta dodge! Rubin will have planted explosives all over the place by then and we will blow the shit out of that apartment."

He searched their faces, wanting to be sure they were following along with the instructions before going ahead.

"The explosives will be on a timer," he continued, "so be well aware of the time in case there is a glitch in the plan. If the plan is derailed for whatever reason, I'll trust that you guys will figure something out. I'll be watching and listening. If everything works out, we then hit the road to easy street. You guys clear?"

Jesse and Rubin geared up for battle.

"Fuck yeah!" Rubin said.

"Let's do it!" Jesse said. He exited the car almost immediately.

A car engine roared up to the apartment. Chris sat relaxed in his seat, watching an incoming Lamborghini from the rear-view mirror. Jim Powers sat behind the wheel.

"There he is," Chris said.

Jim pulled forward and turned the corner.

Chris broke into a frenzy. "Shit! Where's he going?"

He looked at the back seat, aiming his question at Rubin.

"He's probably just looking for a parking spot," Rubin assumed. "I'll get out and follow him."

"Be careful and don't let him see you," Chris warned. "Make sure you're back here in five minutes."

Rubin exited the vehicle and sauntered in Jim's direction. Chris peered out through the window, staring after him until he disappeared out of sight, after which he redirected his attention to the apartment complex, his gaze reaching for the unit where Stephanie lived. He stared at her balcony.

***

Jesse crawled into Stephanie's apartment through the bathroom window. He stood flat against the tiled wall and quietly pulled out a knife, grasping it defensively as he inched his way toward the open door. He poked his head out and looked to the left, where Officer Hansen stood admiring a work of art in the living room.

Wanting to make sure the coast was clear, he swiveled his head to the right. A hand gripping a long knife sprang at him, lodging the knife deep into his throat. The knife penetrated the base of his skull, killing him in perfect silence.

The homeless man retracted his knife. He fixated his eyes on the man in the living room; he could vividly recall it was the same police officer who'd burst out of the squad car and chased him down the street. Careful not to earn the man's attention, he dragged Jesse's lifeless body toward the bathtub and shoved it inside.

Smeared with blood, the homeless man drew the shower curtain closed. He grabbed a towel from a hanger and with it he wiped off the blood that had splattered across his face. He returned the towel to its place and quietly locked himself in the bathroom.

***

Officer Hansen strolled to a coffee table where a framed picture sat. He picked up the picture—it was the picture of two young children and a woman in her forties. All three had enviable smiles on their faces. He could tell from their old fashioned clothes that the picture had existed for no less than two decades. The young girl in the picture had a striking resemblance to Stephanie, so he concluded it was her as a child. The boy beside her was undoubtedly her brother, and the woman in the picture had to be their mom.

A knock at the door retracted Hansen's attention from the picture. He returned the picture frame to the coffee table and approached the front door, an aura of confidence around him. Looking through the peephole, he found Jim standing outside, briefcase in hand.

Jim stood rooted to the doorway, surprise flashing across his face as Hansen opened the door. "Officer Hansen! The last time we met was in my limo, as I recall. After our business exchange, I must admit...I'm a bit surprised to see you here."

"Shhh!" Hansen brought his index finger to his lips. His eyes panning the living room, he leaned in close to Jim and whispered into his left ear, "It's not what you think, Jim. I'm on your side. They think I'm on *their* side. You are going to get your daughter back safely and you are going home with that briefcase. Just follow my lead...please."

That said, he leaned away from Jim. He cleared his throat, reached behind and flipped out his gun from where he'd lodged it beneath his jacket. He aimed the gun at Jim, pointing it right between his eyes.

He barked out an order, "Alright, pal, set the briefcase down and hands straight up where I can see 'em!"

Jim calmly placed the briefcase on the floor and suspended his hands in the air.

Hansen swatted the air sideways with his gun. "Spread 'em!"

Jim spread his legs, maintaining his trademark calmness as Hansen frisked him. Finding nothing, Hansen took a tentative step back.

"Daddy!" Stephanie's sobbing voice slithered from the bedroom. Hysterical and shrill, it engulfed the whole house. "Is that you? Please help me...please!"

"That's your daughter, Jim," Hansen said, maintaining his loud voice so Gus could hear. "If you want to see her alive, hand over the briefcase and slowly come inside!"

He leaned in close to Jim.

"Just play along," he whispered.

Hansen received the briefcase, the load it held weighing down his right hand. He stepped aside for Jim to proceed into the living room. Jim cast a weary gaze around the house as he stepped in.

"Turn around!" Hansen ordered. "Flat against the wall!"

Jim complied without a word.

Hansen set down the briefcase and whipped out a set of handcuffs. "Put your hands behind your back, Jim!"

Jim bristled against the wall, apparently now suspicious of Hansen. He made no move to follow Hansen's latest instruction. Just as he started to turn around, Hansen placed his gun to the back of Jim's head, stopping him cold.

"I said hands behind your fucking back!" Hansen's voice flared higher than it ever had.

Stephanie's frenzied screams tore out of the bedroom, "Daddy...Please! Do what they tell you! They are going to kill me if you don't!"

The rest of her words were muffled into an almost inaudible 'mmph!' no doubt resulting from her being silenced with a gagging device. That was enough to force Jim into submission. He held his hands behind his back, letting Hansen slap the cuffs around his wrists.

"I want to see my daughter!" Jim demanded. "Right now!"

"Not so fast, Jimbo," Hansen said in a stern voice. "We need to count the cash first. Sit down on that chair."

He gestured to a single dining room chair sitting in the middle of the living room. Casting him a weary look, Jim walked over to the chair and sat down.

Hansen could feel Jim's gaze piercing through him as he walked over to a duffel bag in the corner of the room. The man's trust was wavering; Hansen could see it in the way he fixed his eyes on him, watching his every move. He unzipped the bag and pulled out a rope and a roll of duct tape. He proceeded to bind Jim to the chair.

● ● ●

"Hey, what—" Jim protested, but Hansen silenced him with a tape to his mouth, then ripped his shirt wide open. "I didn't think you were stupid enough to be wearing one," Hansen said, "but just in case."

CHAPTER NINETEEN

Drained of all energy, a dehydrated David remained chained in the warehouse. The iron chains dug deeper into his skin, leaving burning imprints. His hair, now dampened with a steady flow of perspiration seeping out from his scalp, clung to his forehead and the sides of his face, tickling him. He shook his head to get rid of the locks of hair—no luck. Beads of sweat dripped down the contours of his face, and his whole body was a mess of stale sweat and urine. A few seconds ago, he'd found that ensuring the day-old pressure in his bladder was beyond him, and had relieved himself right there on the floor where he sat.

He wiggled against the chains, desperate to break free, but the locks of iron dug into his skin even more, intensifying the pain. His breath turning ragged, and still he took another shot at it. His muscles strained as though they would burst. He took a breather, panting softly. The others were all gone, and here he was, forgotten. Dying of dehydration, with his nude corpse in a pool of piss and sweat was not how he'd pictured his end. He struggled against the chains again.

"C'mon!" he urged. "C'mon, c'mon! Goddammit!"

Still, the metal didn't budge.

"Fuck!"

The roar of an engine filled his ears as a vehicle halted outside the warehouse. He snapped his head toward the entrance door. Seemed like someone had remembered him.

● ● ●

The car door slammed shut and footsteps shuffled in his direction. Not exactly knowing who to expect, he kept a level gaze. The worst that could happen was him ending up with a bullet ripping a smoking hole between his eyes. And he'd spent the past couple of hours bracing himself for that.

A female burst in through the door, bolt-cutter in hand, and before David could register her face, sweat rolled into his eyes, momentarily blinding him. With the female now locked out of sight, he could only depend on his ears—they carried her hurried footsteps to him. He blinked repeatedly, finally overcoming the saltiness that had overpowered his eyes.

"What are you doing here?" he asked, pleasantly surprised at the sight of Shelly.

Shelly snapped the chains and padlock with the bolt-cutter. "Getting you out."

David furrowed his brows. How had she learned of his capture, and of the exact location he was held hostage?

"Come with me," she said. "I have some clothes for you in the car."

Her words fanned the flames of his confusion. She'd known of his nudity as well. But how?

"How did you—" he started.

"Just come with me!" she said, with palpable notes of urgency in her voice.

David scrambled to his feet. Lightheaded and without an ounce of strength, he made for the exit, but the slippery wetness underneath his feet sent him sliding back toward the floor. Shelly's arms shot out toward him. She gripped him firmly, preventing a disastrous fall. She looked away from him, away from his nudity.

It would mean nothing to David if his employee gawked at him in his sheer nakedness. His nudity was the least of his concern at the moment. If he'd succeeded in breaking out of the chains and had found no piece of clothing in the warehouse, he wouldn't have had any difficulty walking into the nearest residential building to request some clothes. Getting out of here—away from Gus—was his top priority

"Careful," Shelly said, guiding him toward the exit.

***

Hansen set down Jim's briefcase on the coffee table and opened the latches. An ear-to-ear grin crossed his face as he rummaged through stacks of tightly bound one-hundred-dollar bills.

"You're a lucky man, Jimbo. Your old man gets stuffed in a pine box and you walk away a multimillionaire. Must be nice." He approached Jim with a smug smile on his face. "Ya know what isn't nice? Being screwed over by a man in uniform. Someone you trust. Someone who's supposed to be on your side."

Jim's face was a mask of confusion. Hansen could tell the old man was having a hard time trying to figure out whether he'd made a mistake by trusting him, or if this was all part of a plan he had to play along with.

Hansen returned to the briefcase.

"Bring out the girl!" he shouted out to Gus, shutting the briefcase. "The money's all here."

The bedroom door slowly creaked open and Gus moseyed through it, holding Stephanie hostage with a gun aimed at her temple. She was dressed in a plain white top and skin-tight jeans, and was gagged with a bandana. She held her hands behind her—they were bound with a taut, unyielding rope. Gus shoved her forward, forcing her to step further into the living room. His gun's aim never strayed off target.

"Well well well," Gus said in a sing-song voice. "If it ain't Jimmy Powers, Junior. You look really pathetic right about now. Can I just tell you something? I enjoyed every single moment of taking out your father, watching him suffer. Seeing the great Jim Powers, Senior breathe his last breath as I smashed his head in with a brick! I gave him a chance and the old man blew it."

Gus' words hit home. It was no secret Jim was having a hard time controlling his rage. He clenched and unclenched his jaw, glaring at Gus as he clung onto every word.

"Ya know what's gonna be even more enjoyable?" Gus continued. "Taking the money that he left you and then taking off to a foreign land with someone that you love." He paused for a dramatic effect, giving Jim a moment to take a guess. "Someone that you trust."

He untied the bandana, ungagging Stephanie.

A visibly shaken Stephanie glowered at Jim. "You thought it was pretty funny kicking me out onto the streets when I was sixteen-years-old, huh? I didn't ask to get pregnant, it just happened, okay? I lived in my car for eight fucking months! I was beaten and raped repeatedly. The baby never stood a chance. And where were you? Getting high...just like you always have...just like you always will. I hate your fucking guts and will never forgive you for what you put me through!"

Gus smirked behind her. He stroked his clean-shaven chin, enjoying every moment of the unfolding drama. "Before this goes any further, there's something you both should know."

The smirk on his face deepened, taking on a sinister look as he turned to address Stephanie. "Your date the other night...Mitch. That was your brother who went missing twenty-some years ago." An overwhelming silence fell upon the room. "Yeah, I know," Gus continued, "they changed his name. It was Scott, right?

Stephanie turned pale as a ghost as she processed the news. And while she did, Hansen recalled the evening he'd found her standing beside a puddle of blood at an alley. The look on her face was a replica of the expression she'd worn when he first met her.

"Remember when I asked if he looked familiar?" Gus asked.

Although Stephanie was too wounded to speak, a blink of her eyes as she acknowledged Gus' question was all he needed for an answer. And from the detached look in her eyes, it was easy to deduce she was deep in retrospection.

"That was me trying to get a reaction," Gus said. "But like I suspected, you didn't have the slightest idea why he looked so familiar. By the way, how did it feel walking your long lost brother to his death?"

Leaving her to reflect on his words, he turned his attention to Jim. "Your wife never forgave you for taking your eyes off him that day at the park, did she? Sad she never got to see him come home." He punctuated his words with a chuckle.

Jim's internal rage escalated. He gritted his teeth and clenched his fists. A glower crept into his eyes, but it wasn't aimed at Gus. His focus was elsewhere—at the plain wall. It was obvious he was lost in a sea of memories.

Stephanie was in complete shock. The deepening hollow between her shoulder blades suggested she was holding her breath. Perhaps this was her way of holding back from dissolving into tears. But it didn't take long for her glistening eyes to overflow with tears, leaving fresh tear tracks on her cheeks. She'd barely even moved a muscle since Gus' grand revelation.

Gus returned his attention to her. "Now, Steph...I know what you're thinking. But trust me, I had to do it. We didn't need your brother interfering or coming after his share of the family fortune if he ever found out he was kidnapped and came from money. It was bound to happen eventually. You can thank me later."

***

A duffel bag bursting with explosives dropped into Stephanie's bathroom through the window. A heavy thump followed right after. The homeless man stayed crouched on one side of the bathroom vanity unit. Stealthy as a shadow, he pulled out his knife and grasped it firmly. He waited for footsteps, but he heard none. Apparently Rubin, who'd just snuck in, had paused at the sight of the smears of blood on the floor.

The homeless man stayed still for the next few moments, after which he peeked from atop the vanity unit, watching the man edge toward the bloody shower curtain. Gun drawn, the intruder wearily made his way to the curtain. He threw it open and found his partner's corpse sprawled out in the tub.

"What the—" he shrieked.

He turned around just in time to have a knife rammed into his ear. The homeless man retracted the knife. He plunged again—this time, his knife found Rubin's throat, slashing it wide open. Blood splattered across the homeless man's face and shirt, smearing all over him.

Rubin's lifeless body slumped to the floor, painting himself red with his own blood. Retrieving the fallen gun, the homeless man edged toward the living room, with his back flattened to the wall.

"I'm taking the briefcase!" he heard Hansen say.

"Are you fucking insane?" Gus' voice followed. "What the hell are you doing?"

"I said I'm taking the Goddamn—" Hansen started, but a bullet to his forehead shut him up.

He collapsed with a thud.

Gus' curious eyes panned the room, trying to connect the pieces. Eyes locked on him, the homeless man shuffled out of hiding, gun smoking.

Gus patronizingly laughed at the sight of him. "We meet again. Don't worry, pal...your dog's safe an—"

In no mood for chitchat, the homeless man aimed his gun at Gus. "Shut the fuck up! Where is he? If I don't see him within the next ten seconds, I will blow all your fucking heads off. All of you!"

A weighty object smashed through the sliding glass door, sending shards of glass everywhere. The homeless man's heart warmed up with an overwhelming emotion as he recognized the four-legged mass of fur. Rex.

Rex hurled himself toward Gus who aimed his gun at him. The homeless man's eyes widened with surprise. He squeezed the trigger, aiming to take down Gus before Gus fired a round at Rex. But all he got was a click—he'd run out of bullets.

With a wry smile, Gus slowly squeezed the trigger.

A shot reverberated around the whole house.

And after it came a moment of silence.

Blood streaked out of a hole drilled into the side of Gus' head. It snaked down his neck, disappearing into his collar and instantly dampening his shirt. He collapsed to the floor, bringing David into sight. David stood at the front door, his smoking gun still aimed at Gus' immobile body. He acknowledged Jim who sweated profusely, tied to a dining room chair in the middle of the room. Jim shut his eyes and inhaled deeply.

"Thank you," the homeless man said to David. "You saved my dog's life."

He pulled out a leash and gestured Rex over.

"Come on, boy! " he said. "Let's go."

● ● ●

Rex raced to his side, tail wagging. The homeless man attached the leash to Rex's collar.

"Sit." The homeless man patted Rex into submission. "Stay right here, boy."

He tossed his gun to the floor and crossed the living room to meet Stephanie. Her eyes were wider than they'd ever been, flaunting her fear. She took a staggery step back.

"Please don't hurt me!" she pleaded. "Take the money...all of it."

"I don't want the money," the homeless man said. "I just want my dog. You promised me you'd help me find him. You lied to me."

"I am so sorry. Really. I took great care of Rex. He's a really great dog." Slow, desolate tears found Stephanie's cheeks. She sniffled, her eyes drooping with sadness as she stared at Rex. Riddled with emotion, she addressed Rex, "So long, Rex. You are back with your daddy now. I'll miss you."

Rex edged toward her and licked her tears dry.

"God will forgive you," the homeless man said. He glanced at Jim, then added, "You should forgive your dad."

***

Stephanie seemed to ponder the homeless man's words as she stared at her father. Maybe she had to forgive him for her life to finally have meaning again. Years had passed and he probably regretted kicking her out on the streets. Holding on to his wrongs would only leave her embittered against him—the only family member still alive. She couldn't deny that at some point there'd been good times with her father, and memories of those days always sought to turn her mushy when she entertained them in her head.

Eyes glistening with tears she held back from shedding, she watched the homeless man and Rex exit the apartment. Once they were out of sight, her face hardened and she looked down at the two guns lying on the floor. The one belonging to the homeless man was unloaded, she looked over to the gun in Gus' grip.

She motioned to David. "Take him out."

"Who?" David asked, confused.

"My dad!" Stephanie gestured at Jim who remained unmovable in the chair. "Take him out! You and I will split the money. Just do it!"

David's brows knitted in concentration as he considered Stephanie's juicy offer. He walked over to Jim and peeled off the duct tape from his mouth.

Jim gasped. "Stephanie...don't do this. What happened between us is water under the bridge. Let's just put everything behind us and try to move on with our lives. If you want the money, take the money. It means nothing to me. You mean something to me."

David yanked Gus' gun out of his death-grip. Facing Stephanie, he said, "If you want to take him out, do it yourself."

He proceeded to untie Stephanie. Puppy-eyed, she stared at him as he pressed the cold metal of the gun into her palm. She reluctantly wrapped her fingers around the gun.

"Not so fast, Satin Damsel," a voice boomed from the doorway. "Not so fast."

Stephanie gasped with disbelief as she found Chris standing in the doorway. His eyes, just like his gun, were fixated on David.

"Drop your weapon," he ordered.

David slowly dropped the gun and raised his hands in the air.

Chris spat out another line of command, "Turn around and slowly walk backward toward Stephanie! Keep your hands where I can see 'em!"

Once again, David complied.

"Okay," Chris said, "Stop!"

David halted between Jim and Stephanie—he had his back to her.

Chris spoke again, "Gentlemen, I despise you both. You each know why. I hope you both rot in hell for what you've done. Jim, I'm not quite done with you. David, it's time to meet your maker. Steph, take him out."

Stephanie aimed her gun at the back of David's head. She slowly squeezed the trigger, releasing a shot. In the split-second that the bullet whizzed toward David, Shelly jumped into view and tackled him to the ground. Dazed, Stephanie could only gawk at her. She had no idea where Shelly had burst out from. Shelly and David lay unscathed on the floor.

Stephanie's haze cleared just enough for her to realize she'd just put a bullet through her father's head. Jim's bullet-stricken head flopped forward, with thick blood oozing out onto his shirt.

Stephanie stood trembling, too shocked to process what had just happened. She unclenched her hands, and the weapon clanged against the floor. The clang sounded far-off, like the fading memory of a dream. Reality seeped into her, hitting her full force she collapsed to her knees.

"No!" She cried hysterically, pummeling the floor as the flames of guilt invaded her bones.

The closet door slowly opened, and Melissa waltzed out, gun drawn. "Nice work, Shelly."

Melissa aimed the gun at Shelly and put a bullet through her head, exploding the back of her head into a mess of blood and brain matter.

"David, Stephanie, get up!" Melissa gestured at them with her gun. "Both of you!"

David and Stephanie slowly rose to their feet. Melissa redirected her aim, placing Chris on the receiving end of the gun.

"Chris, drop the fucking weapon or I swear to God, I will blow your worthless brains out right now!" she ordered, her strident voice leaving no room for sluggishness.

Chris tossed his gun to the floor and raised his hands in the air.

"All three of you...over in the corner. Keep your hands where I can see them." Melissa aimed her gun at David. "Screw me once, shame on you. Screw me twice, shame on me."

She took him out with a bullet to the chest. With a face radiating pure evil, she stared coldly at Chris and Stephanie.

"How ironic that the two of you stand before me after screwing around with your cyber-love-affair behind my back," she said, her voice holding a barely palpable note of amusement. "Too bad you never got to fuck her, Chris. It's as good as you'd imagine."

Melissa's words sent images of their bedroom sounds flooding Stephanie's head. It brought her attention to the soreness Melissa had conjured up between her legs. Her stomach churned at the memories overwhelming her. But she knew her lost dignity was not the most reasonable thing to worry about at a time like this.

Melissa aimed her gun at Chris. Her eyes narrowed to slits and she grit her teeth.

● ● ●

Chris held out his hands in a 'stop' gesture. He took a wobbly step toward Melissa. "Melissa...don't do anything stupid. Let's talk about—"

Melissa pulled the trigger, blowing his head off. Stephanie shrilled in horror. She jumped backward, narrowly escaping Chris' corpse as it toppled with a shuddering thump. Now the last one standing, she looked up to find Melissa's gun aimed at her head.

"Steph, what can I say?" Melissa asked. "You got me a job and I'm extremely grateful for that. You also tried to lure my husband away, you led your brother to his demise, and you just killed your own father. And for what?"

Her eyes followed Melissa as she shuffled toward the coffee table and lifted up the briefcase.

"Everything you do, you do for this. It's mine now, all of it." Melissa returned the briefcase to the coffee table and grasped her gun with both hands.

"Oh, God. What have I done?" Stephanie clenched her face with trembling hands. She sobbed uncontrollably, her body quavering with every gasp and hiccup.

She uncovered her face just in time to see a near-orgasmic expression on Melissa's face. Melissa slowly squeezed the trigger. Stephanie held her breath, waiting for the end to come.

A gunshot ripped into her ears.

She froze.

Melissa's face suddenly paled, and time seemed to slow down as she collapsed. Blood gushed from her head, instantly pooling around her. Stephanie gasped, her gaze darting to the doorway. The homeless man had come to her rescue. Gun in hand, he stood with Rex at the doorway.

Shuddering, Stephanie examined the carnage all around her—bodies, weapons, death, greed, sin. She stood in

• • •

paralyzing silence, gazing at the homeless man with tremendous guilt.

***

The homeless man had been on his way out, but resounding gunshots had informed him of a need to save the lady who'd kept Rex safe. He held Stephanie with his soft gaze. He soothed her with his eyes, wordlessly comforting her with his presence, his warm eyes. Everything would be alright; all he wanted her to do was believe, to let go of the guilt and flip to a new chapter of her life.

Stephanie broke her gaze and wandered aimlessly around the living room. She doubled over and retrieved a firearm.

"You don't need that," the homeless man said. "I'm not going to hurt you."

"You don't understand!" she said, her crying voice on the brink of incoherence. She waved her gun around. "Look around. Do you see the damage I've done? Everyone I've ever loved is dead and it's all my fault."

Her fingers slowly found the trigger.

"Please, put the weapon down," he said. "It's all over now."

Stephanie shook her head vigorously. She squeezed her eyes, forcing out rivulets of tears. In a swift move, she spun the gun around, holding it against her temple.

"Please," the homeless man said, "you don't have to—"

Desperate to save her, he started toward her, but the blare of a gunshot stopped him in his tracks. Stephanie's head exploded into a sea of red, splashing against the wall behind her. Rex howled in sorrow as her body pummeled to the floor. The homeless man's chin sunk into his chest, and a single teardrop rolled out of his eye. He shook his head, disbelieving.

Walking around corpses and blood, he made his way to the coffee table where Jim's contentious briefcase sat. He opened the briefcase and examined its contents—it was stacked with hundred dollar bills. With an assertive nod, he closed the briefcase.

"Let's go, boy," he said to Rex.

Briefcase in hand and Rex by his side, the homeless man contentedly vacated the apartment. He'd only taken a few steps into the street when a blinding burst of light engulfed the apartment as it erupted into a ball of fire and smoke. With the flames came a total silence that could only have resulted from the deafening sound of a mistimed bomb detonating. The homeless man walked on into the distance, never sparing a second to look over his shoulder at the apartment as it reduced to ashes.

EPILOGUE

The homeless man strolled through the tranquil, lush grounds of a cemetery. Briefcase in hand, he walked between rows of tombstones. The cemetery was flanked by tall trees which swayed to the tune of the wind, shedding their leaves across the ground. Rex was alongside him, matching his snail's pace. A single long-stemmed red rose lay lodged in Rex's less-than-delicate mouth.

The homeless man stopped in front of a particular grave. His gaze dropped to the tombstone's inscription:

'Here lies Jim Powers, Senior. Devoted husband, loving father, faithful Christian and philanthropist. May his loving soul rest in eternal piece in the loving arms of the Lord.'

"I believe this belongs to you," he said, draping the briefcase over the grave.

He plucked the red rose from Rex's mouth and placed it over the briefcase. He looked up at the heavens, noting how gloomy clouds blanketed the earth with a slowly-building darkness. Thunder rumbled overhead, and the trees swayed more vigorously.

The homeless man took this as his cue to leave. He took a step back.

"Let's go, boy," he said to Rex.

Rex barked in response. The homeless man whistled peacefully as he and Rex crossed into the sunset.

While his whistling voice and his receding footsteps faded into the distance as he walked further away with Rex, a human arm shot out from beside Jim Senior's grave. The person's fingers hid beneath a brown leather glove that extended over the long sleeve of a trench coat. The gloved hand locked its fingers around the handle of the briefcase, gingerly heaving it off the grave.

And the only witness to the theft was the setting sun.

Made in the USA
Columbia, SC
23 August 2023

22031567R00098